Coaching Rugby League

also by Ray French

My Kind of Rugby: Union and League

COACHING RUGBY LEAGUE

Ray French

Foreword by David Oxley
Secretary-General, Rugby Football League

Preface by Maurice Oldroyd
National Administrator, British Amateur Rugby League Association

Line drawings by Ken Tranter

Approved by the Rugby Football League, the British
Amateur Rugby League Association, the Universities
and Colleges Amateur Rugby League Association
and the English Schools Rugby League

faber and faber

First published in 1982
by Faber and Faber Limited
3 Queen Square London WC1N 3AU
Printed in Great Britain by
Fakenham Press Limited, Fakenham, Norfolk
All rights reserved

British Library Cataloguing in Publication Data

French, Ray
  Coaching Rugby League
  1. Rugby football coaching
  I. Title
  796.33'3'077   GV945.75

  ISBN 0–571–11954–9
  ISBN 0–571–11955–7 Pbk

Contents

Acknowledgements

I am especially grateful to Brian Middlehurst for his advice throughout the writing of this book and particularly for his constructive criticism of the finer points of coaching Rugby League. His generous contribution has been essential to whatever merits this book may possess.

R.F.

For permission to include photographs the publisher's thanks are due to the following agencies: Aaron Agencies Studio (15); Mike Brett (11); Philip Callaghan (3); County Press Photos (9, 14, 23, 28); George Herringshaw and Associates (2, 20); John Mounfield (17); *The Rugby Leaguer* (22); South Lancs Newspapers Picture Service (1); Andrew Varley (cover illustration, 18); G. Webster (7, 12, 13).

Foreword

Rugby League is an expanding sport. Each new season sees more players enjoying the game on the field and an ever-increasing number of spectators following it from the terraces. This resurgence of interest has brought with it a welcome growth in the general literature on the game. However, for over thirty years, there has been a complete dearth of material concerned with the vital function of coaching. This book will do much to fill this void.

Where the growth of any game is concerned, it is impossible to over-estimate the importance of the coaching effort in all its aspects. The coach is teacher, guide, motivator and tactician. He bears a great responsibility for the all-round development of players at every level. The subjects covered in this volume have undoubted application in the professional game. Individual, positional, unit and team skills, how to make training sessions enjoyable, the use of time and the deployment of resources, motivation and man-management—these are fundamentals about which one simply cannot know too much.

Lively and readable, this book inevitably contains many of Ray French's personal observations on the modern game and will give both players and spectators an insight into its skills and tactics. The reader will find these thought-provoking and, no doubt, controversial. This can only be to the good. The time to worry will come when people no longer think deeply about Rugby League, or bother to argue its issues, for then no one will care. Ray French's stimulating book is eloquent evidence of this concern, and I welcome its publication as a very valuable addition to Rugby League's growing library.

Finally, I must pay tribute to Shopacheck, loyal friends of Rugby League for many years, for their initiative in sponsoring this book.

David Oxley
Secretary-General,
Rugby Football League

Preface

With Rugby League now widely accepted as one of the fastest-growing sports in the country, this is undoubtedly the time to launch Ray French's *Coaching Rugby League*. I am confident that this much needed book will be well received at all levels of the amateur game, where there is a genuine thirst for knowledge and literature on this most important aspect of our sport. Ray French is a true rugby man, in the widest sense, and his deep knowledge and enthusiasm show through constantly in his writing, which has been geared primarily to the schoolboy, university and amateur Rugby League game.

It has been said of many sports that there is too much emphasis on coaching, with well drilled automatons as the end product. Pleasingly, Ray's book always places the emphasis where it should be, namely, on the expression of natural talent and flair for the sheer enjoyment of player and supporter alike—which is surely the essence of amateur sport.

The Coaching Advisory Committee, whose members are drawn from all sections of the game, has given its wholehearted support to this first-class book, which has been approved and recommended by BARLA, by the Universities and Colleges Amateur Rugby League Association and also by the English Schools Rugby League.

Maurice Oldroyd
National Administrator,
British Amateur Rugby League Association

Key to the Diagrams

 Scrummage

F.	◯	Forward
H.	◯	Hooker
P.	◯	Prop
S.R.	◯	Second-row
L.F.	◯	Loose-forward
B.	◯	Back
H.B.	◯	Half-back
S.H.	◯	Scrum-half
S.O.	◯	Stand-off
W.	◯	Wing
C.	◯	Centre
F.B.	◯	Full-back
A.H.B.	▢	Acting half-back
R.	△	Referee
	⊕	Ball

——————→ Player running with ball

– – – – – – –→ Player running without ball

·················→ Player passing ball

⊕- - -⊕- -→ Player kicking ball

1. Introduction

Interest in Rugby League has grown remarkably in recent years. For example, three new professional teams were admitted to the Rugby Football League during the 1980–82 seasons. The British Amateur Rugby League Association (BARLA), a body which Dick Jeeps, chairman of the Sports Council, has described as the sporting success story of the seventies in Britain, now looks after well over 400 clubs, many of them fielding five or six teams. The Universities and Colleges Amateur Rugby League Association, affiliated to BARLA, has nearly twenty member clubs. The English Schools Rugby League, an autonomous body also affiliated to BARLA but financed by the Rugby Football League, caters for some 65,000 schoolboy players. This tenfold increase in the number of school and youth teams, the life blood of any sport, together with the increase in leagues and cup competitions at all age levels, testifies to the growing popularity of this amateur sport.

Equally striking has been the geographical spread of the game. The traditional areas of Lancashire, Yorkshire and Cumbria still remain the strongholds, but popularity has grown in southern England, especially in the Greater London area, as well as in the North-East, the Midlands and even Wales and Scotland.

For player and spectator alike Rugby League is a fascinating game—a hard, physical confrontation between two teams, combined with skilful ball-handling and running. It has ingredients that few other sports possess. It is essential that those coming fresh to the game, whether they are schoolboys, students, or adults, learn the correct techniques, skills and tactics. Above all, they must learn to develop and express their talents in an uninhibited way so that the game remains enjoyable to play and exciting to watch.

Coaching Rugby League is intended for schools, universities and colleges, and junior and senior amateur clubs. I hope it will also be of use to a number of professional clubs. There has been no coaching manual since Leeds and Hunslet Schools published their *Manual of Rugby League Coaching* in 1948, and given the changes of recent years it is vital that all those concerned with the game take stock of those developments.

Alongside the actual growth of Rugby League have been changes in the laws which have had a profound effect on the way the game is now played. Of these the most significant has been the six-tackle law which limits the number of times a team in possession of the ball can be tackled before a scrum is awarded to give the opposition a chance of winning the ball. The law was introduced in the 1966/67 season to stop one side monopolizing the play. Originally it allowed for four tackles, but in 1972 this was amended to six. The irony of this law is that there are now fewer occasions—not more as intended—for a player to show his individual skills. This has resulted in a need for an even higher standard of individual skills than previously because a player has to exploit the slightest opportunity in a match to set up try-scoring possibilities. The subtle probing and waiting game with a team retaining possession for long periods is a thing of the past. Consequently, as the emphasis upon certain skills and tactics has changed, it has become necessary for coaching methods to adapt and develop according to the present-day needs of the players, even though many of the basic skills have stayed the same.

In fact, some headway has already been made with the creation and development of various coaching committees, each one responsible for the organization of courses catering for the requirements of the amateur and professional sections of the game. But there is a dearth of publications to help the many coaches and players who genuinely recognize the need to re-appraise the way the game is played. I hope this book will rectify the situation, stimulate new ideas, and give confidence to those trying them out.

Coaching Rugby League will also be of value to the new coach or player, possibly from the world of Rugby Union, and particularly from those areas where the League game has not been played before. The differences between the codes are not as great as they might at first seem. The handling and passing, especially by the backs, is the same; the running and tackling are alike; while the kicking in League still has much to learn from the Union game. Therefore, the convert can approach the new code secure in the knowledge that there is a large area of common ground. At the same time he must also be aware of the skills and tactics peculiar to League, particularly the play-the-ball and its dominating role in shaping attack or defence.

Anyone using this book must obviously be fully acquainted with the rules as set down in the *International Laws of the Game and Notes on the Laws*, obtainable from the Rugby Football League, 180 Chapeltown Road, Leeds. This concise booklet is essential to player and coach alike, particularly as it explains how the laws should be interpreted.

Probably the most important function *Coaching Rugby League* can have is to stir the interest of youngsters in the possibilities of League football. Some observers bemoan the decline of individual skills and it is obvious that if such a decline has taken place (though there is much evidence to suggest that it has not), then more attention ought to be paid to them in the early days of a player taking up the game. It is more difficult to rectify faults later. If League is to continue to flourish, it is the young player who must be encouraged to develop the correct skills and techniques. Yet it is also the responsibility of the coach to see that he is taught properly.

There are considerable difficulties in providing a coaching

1. Rugby is about scoring tries. There is no concealing the delight shown by Jeff Gormley as he scores for the amateurs Pilkington Recs. against Castleford in the first round of the 1978 Rugby League Challenge Cup.

manual to satisfy the demands of all coaches and players, not least because of the large age range of the players and the variations in their levels of experience. Youngsters are usually more receptive to new ideas than older players who tend to become set in their ways. The best way to teach an eleven-year-old, for example, is to stretch his ability as far as possible, and it is surprising how quickly he will grasp what might be thought a difficult concept. He may find some exercises and techniques hard to grasp, so initially they might need to be modified, but once he has mastered them his confidence will soar.

If used creatively, this manual will help player and coach to get more out of the game. Its aim is to encourage greater preparation and organization for matches without losing sight of rugby's basic objective—the scoring of tries. A thrilling, competitive spectacle, after all, is by far the best way of attracting new players and drawing more spectators.

Finally, I must explain that throughout the book I have used the expression 'try-line' instead of the officially correct term 'goal-line'. Experience has taught me that youngsters respond immediately to the more vivid expression 'try-line'. On the other hand, I have expressed distances in metric measurement (as set out in *The International Laws of the Game*, published by the Rugby Football League) rather than in yards, as most adult spectators perhaps would expect, mainly because every Rugby League-playing country now officially uses metric measurement and also because most youngsters in this country already think and work naturally in metric terms.

2. Individual Skills

Rugby League is essentially a team game, with each side of thirteen players endeavouring to score more points than their opponents. Therefore, it is obvious that the success of any team depends on harnessing the individual skills of all the players into an effective collective unit; and the ultimate demonstration of these skills should be seen at international level. Unfortunately, it appears that our top players now lack the individual skills that were expected of their predecessors. This decline, if decline it is, may well result from the lack of attention paid by some young players to the development of individual skills when they are first introduced to the game.

Great Britain has always tended to rely on ball-handling skills, whereas the Australians, our greatest adversaries, have generally placed greater emphasis on supreme physical fitness. Before the introduction of the four-tackle law, and subsequently the six-tackle law in 1972, Great Britain won sixty per cent of their games against the Australians over a period of sixty years. Following the implementation of the six-tackle law the success rate dropped dramatically to about thirty-five per cent. This is surely a reflection of the amount of time spent at both amateur and professional level on developing individual skills. No longer are our individual skills capable of compensating for the Australians' superior fitness.

Coaches should therefore hold training sessions for individual players so that basic skills can be practised and improved and faults rectified. Closer attention to individual skills will not only add to the spectacle and excitement of the game for the spectator, but will build up a player's confidence in himself and encourage him to display his talents on the field.

Physical strength and speed of movement are two of the most crucial elements in League, but the scoring of tries often depends upon the quality and speed of passing. Preventing tries necessitates solid and correct tackling of an opponent. The crux of the game, therefore, is about one individual's skills triumphing over another's more limited abilities (though obviously allied to the rest of the team effort). Unlike Union which has a greater number of elements demanding the application of unit skills—scrum, line-out, ruck and maul—the League game tends to be a more individual one, having only three areas of unit skills—the scrum, the play-the-ball, and the tap penalty.

PASSING

In a handling game as fluent as League, all players, forwards as well as backs, are expected to give and to take a pass with equal facility. And since most tries are scored after an overlap or gap has been created, the skill of passing must surely be the most fundamental in the game and one not to be neglected by a coach. Ideally, he should keep all his team together when practising this so that the players are used to handling the ball among themselves. This will also provide the opportunity for practising the different types of pass that often have to be made by players in particular positions.

A player should always try to make the ball do the work for him, and the two key factors in moving a ball from A to B as quickly and effectively as possible are *speed* and *accuracy*. Speed does not necessarily mean speed of foot, but rather speed and timing of the pass which will place a colleague who receives the ball in a better attacking position than the passer.

Unfortunately, when describing how to pass, too much emphasis has been attached to foot placements, the swivel position of the body and the turn of the waist. Most skills are performed naturally and all of these elements will occur instinctively if the player giving the pass looks at the man to whom he is passing. Coupled to this, a player must develop the art of knowing *when* to make the pass—*timing*. He must be able to absorb quickly what the opposition is doing and then decide whether to pass immediately or to draw an opponent and flick a pass at the last second so the receiver can benefit from the gap created.

Physical size and strength are not important; judgement is. So even a small player with good handling skills and the sense to know when to pass can create try-scoring chances for bigger forwards or backs when close to the try-line. Such skills are priceless and must be encouraged.

Basic Pass

A coach must stress to his players how vital it is to have relaxed arms and supple wrists when giving and taking a pass. When a player has gripped the ball comfortably, with his fingers splayed out underneath and his thumbs exerting a slight downward pressure on either side to retain control, then he is ready to pass. If a player's wrists are supple enough he should be able to rotate the ball in his hands when his arms are held loosely away from his body. There is no need for the elbows, which are obviously bent, to be very close to the player's side, as some would suggest. Though many coaches maintain that the power in the pass comes from the movement of the arms across the body, it is more likely that the direction and control of the ball is provided by the flick of the wrists, assisted by the two little fingers of each hand on either side underneath the ball.

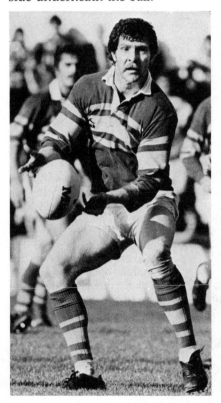

2. When making a pass, it is not just the swing of the arms that gives momentum to the ball, but also the flick of the wrists and little fingers of both hands just as the ball is released. The technique is second nature to players of the calibre of John Holmes (Leeds and Great Britain). Note how his eyes are fixed on the point where he intends to pass the ball.

The receiver should accept the pass away from his body so that the ball can be transferred to the next player in the line at speed. It is important to stress that the ball should be kept at the fingertips, for this will allow the next pass to be given quickly as well as allowing the player to develop an instinctive 'feel' for the ball which is only gained through the fingers. A player should only clutch the ball close to his body if he is attempting to drive hard through a tackle when clearing his own line, or is crashing through a gap in an attacking burst. Hugging the ball close to the body will slow down any passing movement and restrict the options the player has open to him when he eventually decides to pass. Whenever a player moves upfield, the ball should normally be carried in both hands about chest height so that it can be passed easily should the opportunity arise. The passer must propel it a metre in front of the receiver so that he bursts on to it at

3. A player should be encouraged to carry the ball in both hands, chest-high. This will enable him to pass easily to either side or to make a dummy pass. The player therefore keeps his options open and the opposition guessing as to which way he is going to take the play. Here the hooker David Ward (Leeds and Great Britain) shows the correct way to run with the ball, and at the same time he is looking for support players to pass to.

4. If a player is taught the correct techniques when he is young, he will develop good habits that will stay with him throughout his career. This schoolboy player, representing Salford in the Under-11s' curtain-raiser against Castleford at Wembley in 1981, has resisted the temptation to hug the ball under one arm. Instead he rightly keeps it in two hands in front of him while he looks for support before deciding to pass.

5. Len Casey (Hull K. R. and Great Britain), in a match against Halifax, shows how important it is to carry the ball in two hands. Even though he is being tackled, he is still able to make the ball available for a support player, effectively having taken one of his opponents out of the game.

6. Good technique and determination mean that this Salford schoolboy, playing against Castleford in the 1981 Under-11s' curtain-raiser at Wembley, is able to give a controlled pass despite the impending tackle.

7. The receiver of a pass, in most situations, should try to take the ball at speed. The player making the pass should therefore put the ball in front of him so that he can run on to it. In the 1981 Challenge Cup Final at Wembley, scrum-half Paul Harkin (Hull K. R.) moves the ball away quickly from his Widnes opponents. Note how he is concentrating on the point where he wants his team-mate to take the ball and not at the point where he starts his run.

speed and continues his forward run. If a coach demands that the player in possession looks at the receiver of the ball before and during the pass, then all the bodily movements will occur naturally. All the coach then has to do is to emphasize the use of the wrists and fingers.

The ability to pass with such precise timing that a forward or a half-back can be sent through a gap in the opposing defence, or a wing can be sent hurtling for the try-line after a threequarter movement, can only be acquired from constant exercises which resemble as near as possible match conditions. Regular exercises, and eventually regular match play, are needed to develop the judgement required to give a pass which will place a colleague in a better position or to delay a pass for a split second which will allow the receiver to take the pass at just the right time and speed. A coach can devise a number of ploys and exercises after he has shown the young player how to pass and has got him to practise either with the coach himself or another partner. Exercises must be designed to test not only a player's speed and accuracy of passing but also to create that necessary sense of judgement of when to pass.

Passing Practice—Speed and Accuracy

A keen coach will no doubt have many exercises in mind, or variations of the few listed in this section, in order to develop and enhance his players' skills in passing and receiving a ball. He should also introduce an element of pressure to give his players that sense of urgency in the speed of their passing. But in getting players to move the ball quickly he should not tolerate inaccurate, sloppy or casual passing. An element of competition will also prevent the boredom which can stem from repetitive exercises and which if not dealt with will lead to lapses of concentration. The exercises listed below demand speed and accuracy for they place a player under pressure of time, while the last one will help to develop that sense of judgement and timing as these qualities come under pressure from opponents.

Circle Passing   Divide the players into groups of seven or eight, and make them stand five metres apart forming a circle. The ball should be passed quickly round the circle while the coach stands in the middle encouraging and complimenting good passing. One of the group then has to run round the outside of the circle three times while the ball is passed from fingertip to fingertip. The coach must count aloud the number of passes made as the runner completes the circuits, deducting two passes for every dropped ball. Two or three groups can easily compete against each other to see which can make the most passes.

Line Passing   The simple exercise of having five or six players run up and down a pitch passing a ball along the line will allow the players to get a 'feel' of the ball. But by making them work at speed, greater demands can be made on the accuracy of their passing. Place seven players at equal intervals along the try-line and make them pass the ball four times back and forth along the line while running the length of the pitch. As they do this get four forwards to run a relay along the opposite try-line, with each forward running one width (see diagram 1). The group passing the ball, seeing the runners ahead, must complete four lines of passing before the runners complete their relay. The exercise will prove that the ball can be moved accurately and at greater speed than the runners. The exercise can be made more difficult for the runners with the ball by giving them a certain time in which to complete their stint of passing. Once a length is completed players can change groups to add variety to the exercise.

Link Passing   This is another variation of line passing and will encourage the receiver to back up the player with the ball and to take the pass on the burst. Follow the format of the previous exercise, but this time, after the first player has passed the ball, he has to sprint along the line behind the group to receive the ball from the last man. The ball is then passed back along the line and the movement begun again. With seven players in a line this will demand even quicker and more accurate passing if the movement is to be completed seven times over the length of the pitch. To increase the element of competition the relay team should be increased to six runners. It can be done!

Rugby Baseball   Though this exercise (see diagram 2) will help to round off a training session in a lighthearted manner and provide considerable enjoyment for all involved, it nevertheless is an excellent game for testing many passing skills and other aspects of League. As in baseball or rounders, make up two teams of nine or ten players. The 'fielding' side should spread out round the field, though no one need guard the bases round which the

Diagram 1.

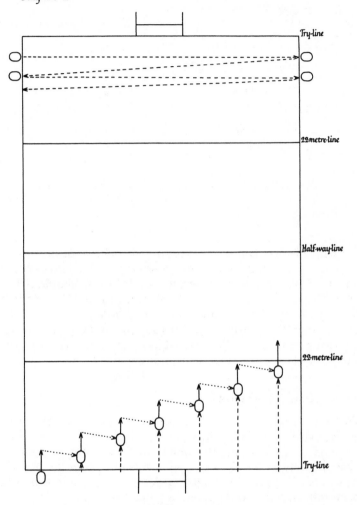

'batsman' will run. The 'batting' side line up to face the 'bowler'
who passes the ball to them in turn. The 'batsman' has to kick it as
far as he can away from the fielders and then run round all of the
bases to gain a run or a point. The fielder nearest to the ball should
either catch or retrieve it, and immediately all the other players on
his side must get behind him so the ball can be passed through the
whole team. If all the passes are made by the fielding side before

Diagram 2.

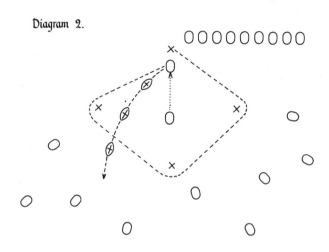

the batsman has completed his run, then he is out. But if he completes his run before all the passes are made, then he scores one point. When three batsmen are out, the teams should change over. This is an excellent game for encouraging the retriever of the ball to look for support immediately and for instilling in the other players that they must provide this support and be ready to form a passing movement. Players will also gain practice in placing shrewd kicks and the regular running will aid fitness.

Passing Practice—Timing

The art of timing a pass is very much dependent on a player being able to 'read' a particular situation in a game and knowing how to respond. Consequently, this ability to know when to make the pass can only be developed if a player is put under the pressure he would experience in a match. So for this reason opposition has been introduced into the following exercises.

Double Passing   Set two groups of players between the try-line and the 22-metre-line (as in diagram 3). The front group should have five players and the second group six. Although the playing positions are marked, they can be taken by any player except the wingers who should retain their positions where they will be given the opportunity to sprint thirty to forty metres. The front group should set off upfield at speed passing the ball down the

Diagram 3.

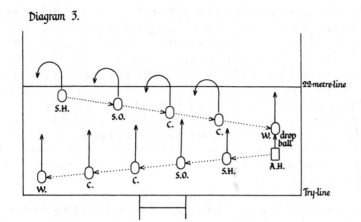

line, followed by the second group fifteen metres behind. When the wing of the front group receives the ball, he has to sprint for thirty metres with the rest of his colleagues trying to keep pace with him. He should then stop to play-the-ball to the following player in the acting half-back position. The second group now transfer the ball along the line while the front group (now only four players) act as a defence. The second line should exploit their overlap by drawing the opposition before making well timed passes. The movement, if performed correctly, should result in the second winger scoring in the corner.

Five against Three Set three players on the try-line beneath the goalposts with five players scattered anywhere between the 22-metre-line and the half-way-line. One of the group of three should kick the ball upfield in the direction of the other five players who should retrieve the ball and set up a passing movement in an attempt to score a try against the three defenders. The attackers will need to time their passes to put a colleague into clear space, and with only three defenders they will have the opportunity to develop the necessary judgement to achieve it. A coach can allow his defenders to tackle or touch the attackers with both hands as a means of stopping the attacking movements.

Passing Practice for Forwards

Forwards and backs must be able to pass as well as each other. Consequently, a coach should be able to place his forwards in all the situations normally encountered by a back. He should also allow his forwards to mingle in a line-up containing backs on either side of them. However, forward play in League often demands handling and passing at very close quarters in confined areas, mainly from a play-the-ball. Two or three passes are often quickly linked together by a set of forwards to try to break through a defence. This could lead to a score from close range, or the play could be opened out to the half-backs and threequarter line who should be coming alongside in support to complete the movement. Therefore, it is a good idea to practise a couple of exercises which will encourage quick thinking and quick passing in a confined space.

Play-the-ball Passing Place three players about fifteen metres in from the touchline (as in diagram 4), one on the 22-metre-line, one on the half-way-line, and one on the far 22-metre-line. Each player should have a ball at his feet ready to play-the-ball at the approach of the acting half-back and the rest of the forwards. When he gets the ball from the first play-the-ball, the acting half-back must pass it to the forwards who should continue upfield passing the ball among themselves. All the forwards must handle the ball at least once before they reach the half-way-line where it is then thrown over the touchline and the acting half-back brings the second ball into play from the second play-the-ball. With a shorter distance to cover to the third play-the-ball, the forwards will be forced to speed up the passing, until at the last play-the-ball they will only have twenty-two metres in which to complete their interpassing. Their speed and accuracy of close passing is therefore being stepped up at every play-the-ball.

Numbers A simple but effective exercise is to place a complete back division along the try-line with the forwards grouped ten metres behind the open-side winger. The backs should transfer the ball at speed along the line until it reaches this player, who, after a short sprint to the half-way-line, stops to play-the-ball to the acting half-back and following forwards. The acting half-back then has to pass the ball to the forwards running at full speed who should complete the length of the pitch, again in a confined width. Each forward should be given a number which the coach calls out if he wants him to receive the ball. The forward in possession will have to weave and dodge, speed up or slow down, in order to pass to the specified player.

Diagram 4.

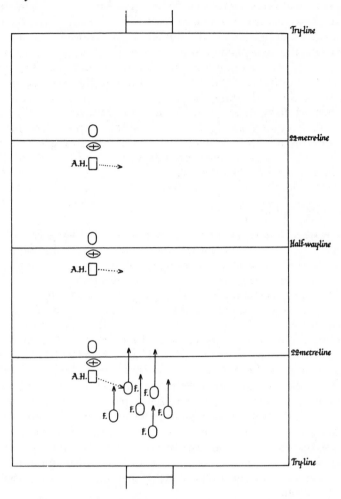

Reverse Pass

Tactically, it is often a good idea to switch the direction of play by making a reverse or back pass to a player running in a different direction. There are two ways of making such a pass; each has advantages and disadvantages. The first method is for the passer to turn his body almost to face the receiver who will have moved inside and behind him. The ball is then simply transferred in the normal manner. The advantage of this technique is that the passer always has the receiver in his sight, but its disadvantage is that it can so easily be recognized by the opposition. The second method is more difficult and demands far greater co-ordination between the two players; but it is more deceptive. The passer remains facing the opponent's try-line as he runs, and then flicks the ball slightly upwards and behind him to the receiver timing his run inside and behind the passer. The ball should only travel a very short distance between the passer and the receiver: the pass therefore requires good judgement by both players. The passer should run directly in front of the receiver, attempting to draw his opponent, while the receiver only crosses behind at the last second when he takes the ball.

The Interception

A daring and risky manoeuvre, but one which adds great excitement when performed by a master, is the art of the interception—a skill which can stop an attacking movement in full flight and turn a defensive problem into a wonderful try.

There are several ways of making an interception. A player can run towards the man he is marking—the player about to receive the ball—and so time his run that he takes the ball almost out of his opponent's waiting arms. In another variation, the interceptor can approach the ball-carrier as if to make a tackle, but at the last instant, as the ball-carrier expects to be tackled, he should move away and take the pass which is often unwisely made.

Making an interception requires experience and the player must have the utmost confidence in his own ability. It should not be attempted too often, but although failure can often end in a try by the opposition, success can bring glory to the interceptor and often victory for his side. On no account, however, should a defending player dodge a crucial tackle by going for an impossible interception.

Dummy Pass

Often a centre in the act of passing the ball to his winger will sense that the receiver is about to be buried beneath an avalanche of covering tacklers. Or a prop forward taking the ball to the open side of the field after a quick play-the-ball movement will realize that there are too many opposition players in front of him, so breaking through the defence is unlikely. In such circumstances, both players can make a dummy pass—the player goes through the motions of making a pass, with exaggerated movements, but just before releasing the ball he draws it back to his body and continues his run. The player making the dummy pass should look at the player who will 'receive' the ball, because his gaze will cause the tackler to look at the 'receiver' as well and so make him hesitate. The dummy pass therefore enables a player to change direction quickly and transfer the ball to an area less well covered by the opposition, or to straighten his run and drive through the gap left by the hesitant tackler. It is a cheeky but valuable weapon in any player's arsenal.

Touch Rugby

The value of touch rugby should never be underestimated as an ideal way of starting or rounding off a coaching session, as the game involves all the players. With a mixture of forwards and backs in each side, a player is 'tackled' if he is 'ticked' (touched). When one side has been 'ticked' six times, the ball should be given to the other side. If a side keeps the ball for a length of time it allows them to probe and set up balanced attacks, and at the same time it keeps a defence at full stretch. It is a worthwhile exercise sometimes to have different numbers in each team, say eight men playing seven, so that one side can try to exploit overlaps by shrewd passing, while the other has to learn to defend when it is outnumbered. The coach should only blow the whistle for a knock-on, a forward pass or when restarting the game and must be sure to keep the two teams ten metres apart. A reduction in the number of 'ticks' is sometimes desirable to stimulate more adventurous play and create greater movement of the ball. Touch rugby should be no easy option, for players must strive and sweat during a session.

Running

Although League is essentially a handling game, there can be far too many passes where the ball is simply transferred from one side of the pitch to the other with little forward movement. Often just by passing for its own sake a player is failing to make a positive contribution to his team's efforts. In effect, without realizing it, he is saying: 'I don't want the responsibility of doing something creative with the ball. I don't want to make a mistake.' When two teams are equally matched, it is often the running skills of one man and the ability to beat his opponent that brings victory and the crowd to its feet. Running skills and the desire to use them must be encouraged in all the players, because if one player can physically beat another it will give him a mental superiority over his opponent and therefore the confidence to play a more prominent role in the game. A winger who deliberately crashes into his opponent and finds the tackle wanting knows he has the beating of him. And a stand-off who deliberately tries to make a break on the outside of his opposite number early in a game in order to test his speed will be instilled with confidence if the defender fails to bring him crashing down in the tackle.

Forwards should be encouraged to develop their running skills, for many can be as adept as the backs, given the right encouragement. A sixteen-stone prop performing a neat sidestep is a thrilling sight, and the change of pace of a loose-forward when breaking from a scrum can deceive the tightest of defences.

The Sidestep

A well executed sidestep will enable a player who is rapidly approaching an opponent to change direction abruptly. He does this by deceiving the defender into thinking he is going to pass him on one side while in fact he wrong-foots him and goes by on the other. The move is carried out by driving one leg into the ground to absorb the forward motion and then driving off this leg as the other one takes a long stride sideways to change direction. Such changes of direction can be worked on in training using various exercises, and the coach should concentrate on the speed at which the player moves away after he has made the sidestep. A good practice is to run down two parallel lines about a metre apart and sidestep from one line to another, changing direction as sharply as possible without losing too much speed.

Many players can become adept at performing a sidestep off either foot and so are able to change direction to either side. This is what players should aim for as a defender can anticipate a move if he knows the limitations of his opponent's sidestep. The runner's normal stride pattern must be sustained: any 'clipping' of his stride before the sidestep immediately betrays his intention. However, to my mind, despite regular practice bringing good

8. A well executed sidestep can wrong-foot defences by quickly changing the direction of play. Mick Morgan, playing for England, drives
powerfully off his left leg to round a covering French opponent and so
bring the play back to his supporting players. He has transferred the ball
to the arm furthest away from the defender, leaving the other arm free
for a hand-off if required.

results, the finest of sidesteppers are born with the skill and carry
it out instinctively.

Sidestep Practice   Place a dozen flag posts at five-metre intervals along the half-way-line with a team lined up on the touchline
facing them. The front player carrying a ball should zig-zag
between the posts to the end, practising the sidestep movement,
and then sprint back to hand over the ball to the next man in the
line who should repeat the exercise. When the players have
mastered the technique of changing direction, the posts can be
brought closer together so the sidesteps have to be quicker and
neater. This can be encouraged further by having two teams
compete against each other.

The Swerve

One of the most exhilarating sights on a rugby field is to see a winger leave a defender trailing in his wake by the clever use of a swerve and change of pace. Therefore, just as a bulkier and larger winger should use a hand-off, so any really fast winger, or even a fast centre, should cultivate a swerve because it can lead to the most important break in League—the outside break—which outflanks the cover.

Regular practice is needed to ensure that a player can perfect the movement. He should slow down as he approaches the defender, feint his body towards him, so causing the tackler to check momentarily, and then accelerate away at top speed. Such a manoeuvre can be practised with or without accompanying players.

Practising the Swerve   Place three flag posts along the touchline, one on the 22-metre-line, another on the half-way-line and the third on the far 22-metre-line. A player can run at each post as he would a defender, feint towards it and then accelerate away. A more realistic exercise is to place a runner with the ball on the corner of the try-line and one touchline, while on the opposite touchline there should be a player on the 22-metre-line and another on the half-way-line (as in diagram 5). These two act as defenders while the ball-carrier sets off upfield to score. With both defenders covering across field the winger must beat both with swerves and changes of pace on his way to the try-line. If he does not beat them, he soon will after a few crunching tackles!

Hand-off

One of the saddest features of the League game today is the dearth of the hand-off. For the forward or big back who has difficulty in changing direction quickly or who lacks sheer acceleration, it can be a powerful asset. A winger or second-row who is trying to run round the cover can propel himself past a defence with a well judged hand-off.

As he approaches the defender, the ball-carrier must hold the ball in the arm furthest away from the tackler with his nearside arm held bent. He should straighten this arm at the last moment

Diagram 5.

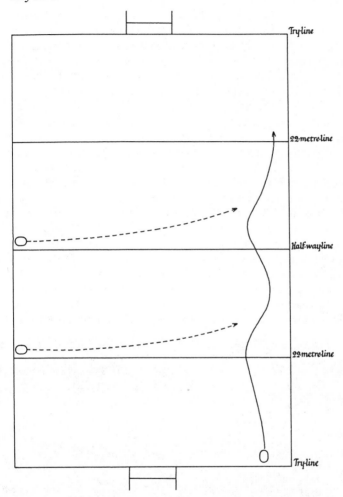

before impact with as much force as possible and push himself
away from the tackler's body with the open palm of his hand. At
the moment of pushing himself away the attacker should launch
into top speed to take him clear of the intended tackle. Coaches
should encourage a big centre or winger to develop the hand-off,
a ploy which can compensate at times for a lack of space in which
to indulge in clever footwork.

TACKLING

While a player must possess many attacking skills, he must never neglect the need of the one basic skill in defence—tackling. Many youngsters relish tackling each other in a game, others shy away from the task, but every player should know how to make and time a tackle effectively. The introduction of the six-tackle law has, I fear, brought about a temporary decline in the art of tackling, for players, particularly forwards, now do not have to make as many tackles in a match as they once did. Consequently the skill has been allowed to deteriorate—this must be rectified! Though youngsters enjoy tackling practices, there is a problem when a coach needs to improve the tackling of adults. Often if players practise tackling in pairs personal duels develop and these are not healthy for team spirit. Therefore, it is best to use tackling exercises for youngsters, and to try to improve the tackling of adults in practices close to game conditions.

The timing of a tackle is all-important. The tackler should move towards the attacker to limit the space, and therefore the attacking options, available. Always on his toes, never on his heels, he will be ready to pounce for the full frontal tackle, which is the most common tackle in League. A coach should stress that the

9. The head-on tackle has to be made more times in a match than any other tackle. By driving forwards and upwards into Eddie Hunter's midriff, Stuart Wright (Widnes and Great Britain) is able to knock his Warrington opponent backwards in a crunching tackle that immediately disrupts a promising attacking move.

tackler drives forward with his shoulder into the waist of his opponent, as if he were going through his body, and with his arms wrapped tightly round him.

A tackle which is much favoured today is the smother tackle. In this the tackler needs to aim higher up the body with the intention of clamping the attacker's arms and covering the ball, thereby stopping any vital pass being made. Such a tackle is made almost standing with the head held high and is more akin to a collision of two bodies accompanied by the vice-like grip of the tackler. This is very effective when defending the try-line as it prevents any sleight of hand putting another player through a gap in the defence. Unfortunately, when overdone, it can lead to sloppy tackling and those awkward times when, with the runner halted but not grounded, the referee is forced to shout 'Held' to conclude the tackle.

With covering tackles the defender usually has to tackle his opponent from the side or from behind. The area to aim for here is the top of the thighs, for the sudden contact will bring the runner immediately to a stop. A low tackle round the ankles by a smaller player can often be the most effective against a bigger opponent.

Tackling is the aggressive and physical aspect of League, and must be learned from the youngest age so that the adult accepts it as something every player has to carry out during a game. The large padded tackling bags which can be set up for boys to run at are ideal to illustrate the demands of a tackle and are a good measure of the forward thrust generated. The gradual progression from using these bags, which are readily available from sports retailers, to games of tackling should be completed long before adulthood, though the bags are also sometimes used by professional clubs, as we used to do at Widnes before a cup tie, to concentrate the mind on the need for sound tackling. There is no substitute for tackling practice in actual match play, but in games such as 'Bulldog' lads will gain considerable expertise in bringing a player down as well as realizing the enjoyment to be gained from making a successful tackle.

Tackling is a skill to be learned when young, but I firmly believe that adults must not neglect it in training. In my own career at St Helens under coach Joe Coan and at Widnes under Don Gullick we regularly had contrived games where the whole emphasis lay on the tackling. And hard sessions they proved to be!

A good idea is to field thirteen players in attack continuously retaining the ball against a pack of forwards and two half-backs in their own 22-metre area. With the coach either shouting the time or counting aloud the number of tackles made, you would be surprised how a spirit can grip the eight defenders and how long they can prevent thirteen players from scoring. If the match is played over five minutes you can be sure the tackles will increase in hardness in the last few seconds as the defence eagerly try to prevent a score. With only eight players, the defenders are given good practice in timing their tackles, a vital factor in a last ditch stand. When the session finishes the coach can reverse the roles by selecting eight defenders from the attackers to see which team can make the most tackles or keep their try-line intact for the longer time.

Tackling Practice

'Bulldog'   Place two boys midway between the 22-metre-line and the try-line facing their colleagues on one of the touchlines. At the signal from the coach these boys should try to cross to the other touchline as the players in the middle try to tackle them. Those who are tackled on each run stay in the middle until there are no more free runners.

One Tackler   Place one tackler between two flag posts, spaced about ten metres apart. Send runners through the posts in quick succession compelling the tackler to tackle each player as he tries to pass him. Call the next runner as soon as a tackle has been completed, even though the tackler may still be on the floor, so he has no time to rest. The tackler will soon learn the need to move forward from between the posts to cut down the runner's options, while the ten-metre space between the flags is sufficiently narrow to stop a wing running away from a prop who may be in the middle.

KICKING

One of the advantages of the six-tackle law has been the re-emergence of the art of kicking in League, to such an extent that the tactical kicker can wield a strong influence in determining the result of a match. A well judged kick is now often a necessity in a game and can prove more effective as an attacking weapon than a series of well timed passes. I say 'attacking weapon'—though, of course, a kick can also be used effectively in defence. An accurate and long kick to touch can set up an attacking position and save a team's forwards a good deal of work, or a high punt upfield can put a full-back under considerable pressure. All players should make some effort to learn how to kick constructively, and it is sad to see in too many professional teams the need to shield the one effective kicker in a side at a play-the-ball while he prepares to kick upfield. If more players could put their trust in a good kick then the game would gain in variety. So a coach should try to use other kickers to deceive the opposition.

The Punt

The punt directly from the hands is the most widely used kick. A player should be looking for distance to touch to take play upfield, or accuracy in making the defending full-back run from one side of the pitch to the other. Obviously a big player should have the strength to kick a ball a good distance, but length is also gained if the ball is held correctly and struck with the foot at the right time. While these skills are being developed, the coach may have to show considerable patience when teaching youngsters the art of kicking.

When making a punt a player should keep his eye on the ball all the time. He should hold it at an angle of forty-five degrees to the ground and then drop it carefully on to the instep of his foot, which should have the toes straight and pointing to the ground. After impact the head and eyes should still be kept low and the foot should follow through the kick. To avoid raising the head too early a player should first count to three.

Emphasis must be placed on the need to follow through the kick, for the action will help gain greater distance. If the ball is being kicked too high in the air, resulting in a loss of accuracy and distance, check that it is being released downwards on to the foot and is not being thrown up for the foot to meet it. The problem can also be caused by raising the head and eyes too quickly.

Punts can be made to relieve a defence near the try-line, and it is not necessary to wait for the sixth tackle before making the kick. A punt after the second or third play-the-ball may well surprise the opposition wings who have not dropped back to anticipate the kick as they would do on the sixth tackle. Exercises to aid the kicking skills are extremely simple—the secret of success is constant practice.

10. (*Above left*) A good punt starts with the ball being held at the correct
angle in the hands before being dropped on to the foot, as shown here by
David Watkins in his playing days at Salford. Note also that his eyes are
fixed on the ball.

11. (*Above right*) The art of the punt. George Fairbairn (Wigan, Hull K. R.
and Great Britain), here playing for England in the World Cup of 1975,
demonstrates how all the elements of the kick should be controlled. His
body is well balanced, with his leg high up following through the kick.
His head is down, and his eyes are fixed on the point where he has made
contact with the ball.

Pairs   Get two players to kick a ball to each other on a full pitch,
each one seeking to drive the other back to his own line by
successful kicks to touch. Each kick is taken from where the ball
lands or where it rolls into touch.

Flags   Set three flags in a row, five metres apart, on the touch-

12. It is vital when punting that the kicker keeps his eyes on the ball and is not distracted by the opposition bearing down on him. Derek Seabrook (Pilkington Recs.) shows admirable concentration despite the closeness of the Australian opposition in the Great Britain v. Australia Under-19s' amateur international at Headingley in 1980.

line. The kicker must aim to get the ball to cross the touchline at each flag after one bounce of the ball.

Drop-Kick

The drop-kick follows the same technique as for a punt except that the foot must kick the ball immediately after it has touched the ground. A coolly taken drop-goal can be a matchwinner and is now more common in the modern game, so each team should develop a nimble player who can prove reliable in a tight situation. The drop-kick for goal has invariably to be made hurriedly as defenders rush at the kicker, usually with arms outstretched to stop the flight of the ball. Therefore, the kicker must raise the ball very quickly by leaning his body a little further back as he makes impact. For accuracy the ball must touch the ground with the top end pointing slightly towards the kicker.

On the other occasions where the drop-kick is used, as at a drop-out beneath the posts or at a drop-out to restart play from the 22-metre-line, then either a long kick can be made by leaning

13. With a drop-kick, the foot should make contact with the ball just after the ball touches the ground. To avoid the possibility of a kick being charged down, the kicker can raise the ball quickly by leaning back a little as he strikes the ball. Note here that Harry Pinner (St Helens and Great Britain) is perfectly balanced and that his eyes are focused on the ball.

further forward and hitting the ball closer to the ground, or a high, short kick can be used by leaning back and striking the ball as when dropping for goal.

Up-and-Under

This celebrated attacking kick can lead to many tries, especially when a hesitant full-back fails to cover the high ball. Rather than aim for length, the kicker must strike the ball as high as possible so that he and others in his team can charge the waiting full-back

14. The up-and-under kick is an excellent means of putting pressure on a defence, particularly if the full-back is known to be uncertain about how to deal with high balls. The ball should be struck high into the air, ideally so that it will drop in front of the opponents' goalposts. This will give the attacking players time to follow up and pressurize the catcher. Note that for greater accuracy the kicker should have a high follow-through and should keep his eye on his outstretched foot until the ball is well into the air, as demonstrated by Bill Ashurst for Wakefield Trinity against Widnes in the 1979 Rugby League Challenge Cup Final.

and almost be on him before he takes the ball, eager to pick up the odd knock-on or bad fumble. It is an excellent ploy near the opposition try-line.

Grubber Kick

A low punt of the ball along the ground and through a quick moving defence will cause havoc and send the opposition scuttling back in their tracks. An occasional grubber kick in attack will stop the defence from coming up too fast; and the kick can often be used by a centre when near the opposition try-line in such a way that the ball 'stands up' for his winger to run on and score (see also pages 49 and 51).

Goalkicks

'Goalkicks win matches' and the prolific kicking of men such as David Watkins (221 goals for Salford in the 1972/73 season) surely underlines the statement. Most goalkickers have their own distinctive styles and their own peculiarities in run up, but if the kicks are going between the posts, then the coach should leave well alone. This is one area where a player can be bogged down by too much talk of technique. However, a coach must be aware of the problems that can arise with the two basic techniques used to strike the ball—namely, the 'straight-on' method and the 'round-the-corner' style.

15. Many goalkickers develop their own method of kicking goals. Steve Hesford (Warrington), for example, has a distinctive round-the-corner style. It is important that his body is well balanced, that his eyes are fixed on the ball, and that the kicking leg follows through after impact.

16. Full-back Peter Knowles (Millom), BARLA player of the year in 1979, shows a similarly well balanced round-the-corner style in the Great Britain v. Papua/New Guinea amateur international in 1979. Note how the non-kicking foot is level with the ball, so that the full force of his body weight is transferred through the ball on impact.

With the 'straight-on' method, once the ball has been placed in a secure hole in the ground or on a divot, the kicker runs up, keeping his head and eyes down, and swings the toe of his boot on to it. With his head inclined, his eyes must remain on the ball and the non-kicking foot must be as near to the ball as possible in order to gain a maximum swing and follow through with the kicking foot. If the ball is inclined away from the kicker, greater distance may be achieved, while a ball leaning towards him will gain height more quickly. This kick is the easiest to learn, but is not so popular now and has given way to the 'round-the-corner' style.

The 'round-the-corner' kick is a much more natural movement and resembles a soccer player taking a corner kick. The kicker runs up at an angle and strikes the ball with his instep rather than his toe, almost nursing it over the crossbar. The problem with this

17. Few players now use the straight-on kick for goal, but one of the leading exponents was Stuart Ferguson (Leigh and Wales) in the 1960s. In this method the player uses a straight run up and strikes the ball with his toe rather than his instep: note too the high follow-through.

method is a tendency to hook the ball round, although once he knows his kicking abilities a player can allow for this curved path of the ball when he takes aim. A good method of practising this kick is to set the ball up on the corner of the try-line and touchline and then attempt to swing the ball through the posts. It is difficult, but a player will soon get a feel of how far his particular technique 'swings' the ball.

3. Positional Skills

Though a coach will attempt to improve or develop the general skills of his players, it is obvious that each position demands its own techniques. Those required by a scrum-half, for example, are glaringly different from those of a prop forward. So a coach should work hard with players on their positional skills.

In looking at the basic needs of each position a coach should not be too dogmatic in his desire to produce the perfect side. He might hope for big centres, but there have been some brilliant ten-stone midfield players, and despite the need for a hard tackling stand-off, there have been some equally gifted players in that position who rarely made a tackle in their careers. It is the blend of players in a team which is all-important. Provided that the majority of the players are sound in their positions, there is room for any gifted eccentric. He is often the player who gives the crowds that extra excitement in a game—flair must never be stifled.

FULL-BACK

The old-established virtues of full-back play—acceleration and sustained pace to time an entrance into the threequarter line, and solid tackling in the last line of defence—are still as necessary as ever. But now the greater involvement of the full-back in the game demands perhaps the most complete array of skills of any player. A full-back should therefore be able to play in any of the back positions because at times during a match he is quite likely to find himself in any one of them.

Foremost among the requirements of any person in this position must be size and strength. Usually a full-back has to make head-on tackles, so he must be able to check a runner's momentum quickly and put him to ground before he is able to pass to a colleague backing up. Likewise, he must be sturdy enough to knock backwards a player going for the line so the momentum of the attacker does not force him over the try-line.

In Attack

The full-back needs to be a shrewd footballer who has the ability to sense immediately the weaknesses in an opposition's cover and has the acceleration to burst into the threequarter line preferably outside the stand-off, or if not, outside the outside-centre or winger. When joining the line he must be prepared to act as a link in giving and taking a pass to provide an overlap for the winger, otherwise he must burst through and take the responsibility upon himself to go for the try-line. Opportunities

18. The full-back in the modern game is truly an attacking player who must take on the responsibility of prising openings in the opposition defence when all his threequarters are covered. Mick Burke (Widnes and Great Britain) is such a player prepared to attack a defence with determined runs. Seen here in the 1981 Rugby League Challenge Cup Final, he is about to score after breaking through the Hull K. R. line.

often arise from a scrum close to the try-line when the full-back can take a pass from the scrum-half on the blind-side in the role of a stand-off.

The full-back must also have a strong kick for it is useful, particularly if the opposition defence has advanced very quickly, for him to put long, raking kicks to touch behind the advancing threequarter line. Such skill can gain much ground for his team and force the opposition to cover back.

In Defence

If a full-back is to instil confidence in the players in front of him, he must be a sound tackler and have the necessary positional sense to anticipate a breakthrough by the opposition.

A full-back should follow the ball across the field, so that he is in a position to stop a break quickly. He should never be more than fifteen metres behind his own defensive line; if he is further back than this a speedy player may make a break to go round him. From this distance, while he is level with the ball, he will be in a position to advance to cut off the break and limit the runner's movement. In the event of facing a strong wind or in muddy conditions, he will need to be deeper to cover any long, raking kicks to touch or to field any high kicks intended to put pressure on him.

With the greater amount of tactical kicking now in the game, it is essential that a full-back catches the ball securely against his chest. Often he will be forced to take a high ball on his own try-line where he will be faced with a hostile opposition. Dropping or fumbling the ball can often be fatal. He must therefore be a confident player, steady on his feet and able to keep his eye on the ball at all times. When catching he must concentrate completely on the ball and not be thinking of what he intends to do, save setting his shoulder to the opposition when the ball is safely clutched to his chest.

A full-back cannot have too much practice in catching a ball, either kicked in the air by himself or a partner, for a good catch under pressure will boost his own confidence and that of the whole team.

CENTRE

Most attacking moves will at some stage involve the centre. So a coach must look for players who have the flair to create openings and breaks, particularly with the skilful timing of a pass, as it is the centre who transfers the ball to and creates space for potentially the highest try scorer of any team, the wing threequarter. Therefore, the mastery of taking and giving a pass under intense pressure is crucial, especially when playing at inside-centre, as are individual running skills, notably the swerve and sidestep. These running skills, allied to speed off the mark and change of pace, are vital in the art of wrong-footing a defender, causing him to check sufficiently for the centre to run outside him and create an outside break. Far too many centres continually attempt to step inside the defender and meekly accept the tackle—the easy option—without testing their opponent's pace on the outside or attempting to stretch the defensive cover across the field.

In Attack

A centre's main aim when his team are attacking must be to create scoring opportunities for his wing outside him. One of the ways he can create the necessary space is to draw the opposition winger towards him and then give out a fast, accurate and well timed pass. Because this will bring play infield away from the touchline, the winger will then have room to round the opposition on the outside. Similarly, such space can be created if the two centres position themselves close together, as their opposite numbers will then have to move in to mark them. If they transfer the ball quickly, the winger again will have space in which to run. The centres can vary their play sometimes by standing further apart to allow the full-back to come into the line.

A centre must learn to run on to the ball and never take it standing still. He should attack the defence with straight and not lateral running which merely carries the ball sideways across the field and crowds the winger into touch. He must always be alert to moves with his inside partners, whether prearranged or improvised, and practise the many ploys available from set-piece play (see also page 67 onwards). The occasional use of the grubber kick to break down a tight defence will often pay dividends as will the longer and higher kick to the corner for his wing partner to run on to and score (see also pages 42 and 51). The number of tries scored by the winger will usually indicate the abilities of the centres.

In Defence

The ability to sight his man quickly and move into the tackle at speed is an essential part of a centre's play. On most occasions he will have to use the smother tackle (see page 35) as this will stop a pass from being made by his opponent. If the centre possesses considerable pace, he can, without ever being drawn out of position, effectively shadow his opponent towards the touchline where the movement can be baulked by an ill-timed pass to the accompanying winger or by the winger himself being forced into touch through a lack of room to manoeuvre.

A centre cannot be impetuous in defence and must act as part of the defensive threequarter line. He must not rush in too fast or delay his approach, and must come up with the rest of his colleagues in a line, without leaving gaps. The whole back line should swing into the opposition like an outstretched arm. Each player must advance slightly to the outside of his opponent

Diagram 6.

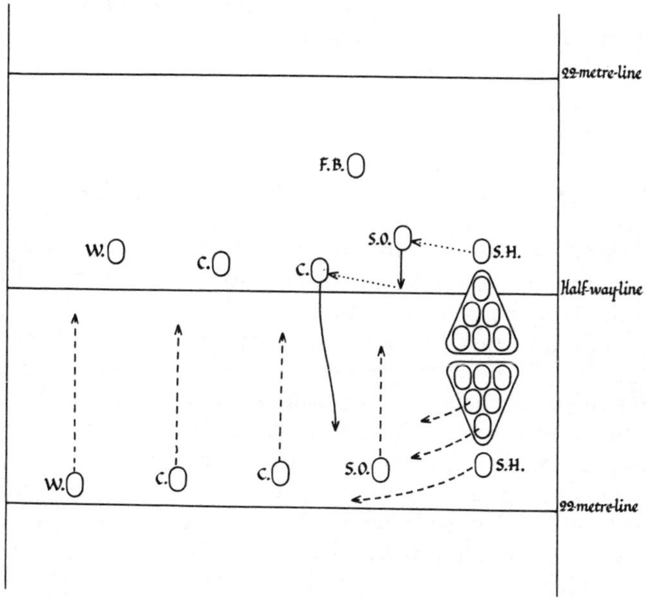

(unless shadowing) so that if anyone is beaten, the opponent will be forced to make an inside break which can be taken care of much more easily by the covering players (see diagram 6). Younger players may find such an operation a little difficult, but it is worth persevering for they will eventually grasp its essentials.

WINGER

It is a sad reflection on the game over recent years that wingers are now scoring fewer tries. Whether this is due to the greater mobility of covering forwards (because there are now fewer scrums in League matches), or to the style of play encouraged by professional coaches, this situation must be rectified, for the excitement of the game largely revolves around the glamour attached to tries scored from the wing position.

Coaches must encourage a style of play which leads to thrilling wing runs, and they should not allow wingers to remain static on the wing merely watching play ebb and flow elsewhere on the pitch. Wingers must be made to earn their keep and not just stand and wait for the ball to reach them. They must be brought into the game at every opportunity so they can use their essential quality—speed. It is also in the interest of other players to move the ball to the winger because when the ball comes back, gaps in the defence can often be found.

In Attack

At the beginning of every match, a winger should quickly weigh up the individual and positional weaknesses of the opposition and adapt his attack accordingly. His speed is clearly his biggest asset, coupled with the sheer desire to score, but he must always vary the way he beats an opponent. A swerve, a sidestep, a hand-off—he must use all his individual skills so that it is difficult for the opposition to anticipate what he is going to do next. Constant practice at taking a pass at full speed will help, as will frequent exercises with his centre, with whom he must develop a perfect understanding. He must always be looking to take a reverse pass, to join a threequarter-line movement by a sudden midfield burst from the blind-side, or to link with the scrum-half on the blind-side of a scrum close to the opposition try-line. He must never stand still to survey what is going on, but should be weighing up the opportunities afforded by his opponents. He might, for example, decide to take a ball in midfield as first receiver from a play-the-ball, and then weave and dodge about among the forward defenders—a ploy which can often cause chaos in the most well organized defence.

As well as being active in passing movements, the winger should also encourage the inside players to kick for the corners in the hope of his outpacing and outflanking the cover to score a try.

In Defence

The winger in defence, moving in quickly to tackle his opposite number as soon as he takes the ball, makes the simplest defensive move to stop a score, particularly if his opponent intends simply to run at or round him. However, if the defending wing is physically inferior to the attacker, but faster, it may be better if he allows his opponent to appear to beat him on the outside and then tackle him from the side round the legs. But care is needed to avoid any intended hand-off. A slower, defensive winger who cannot allow the faster man to take the ball with a running chance will often take the situation into his own hands and dash in from the wing and smother tackle the outside-centre (see page 35). This is an effective but dangerous ploy and one which requires good timing and anticipation. If it works, it can effectively destroy an attacking back movement.

A coach must urge the wing, when on the blind-side, to cover across to stop a movement on the other side of the pitch, or to help stem a forward break down the middle of the field. He must also encourage him to assist a full-back who has had to cover back to field a deep kick. Any switch of direction, by a pass or a dummy pass, can only be covered if the wing races back to assist his colleague in trouble.

HALF-BACKS

Good, cheeky half-backs touch the ball more times in open play than any other player on the field, and because of this, they invariably act (individually or as a pair) as the lynchpin of all the team's attacks, although today a half-back is often used in the role of defensive 'sweeper'. They can dominate a game, and a team with a good pair of half-backs who understand each other's play is well on the way to success. 'Understand' is indeed the key word, for they should practise all their individual skills together so that each knows where the other is when the ball is coming from a scrum or a move has to be worked. Each must learn to anticipate the other's play to such an extent that instinctive, long-lasting partnerships are often moulded.

The half-backs' understanding with their loose-forward is also important and will be dealt with later (see page 69).

Scrum-Half

A scrum-half, like his partner at stand-off, must have pace off the mark. He must not be frail or too small for he must have the resilience and strength, particularly in the shoulders and thighs, to withstand the close attention of forwards round the scrummage and at a play-the-ball. His rugby knowledge must be extensive, for he is the one who is often at the tactical heart of a team, looking for any openings or weaknesses in the opposition. But I am afraid that today the scrum-half seems to have lost sight of his prime function—that of giving a quick pass to his stand-off who will in turn set his back division in motion.

In so many games, balls are heeled untidily from the scrum only to be pounced on and hugged on the ground by the

19. Reg Bowden (Widnes and Fulham) is probably one of the best scrum-halves never to have been capped. His quick service from the scrum gives the opposing loose-forward virtually no time to make a tackle to prevent the ball being moved to the stand-off.

scrum-half, thereby wasting a tackle. This lack of service naturally hampers a team, and is something a coach must work on. The
stand-off should not have to wait for a pass—the ball must reach
him at all cost. If necessary the scrum-half will have to pass from
the ground or throw blind in his efforts to get the pass away. He
should not have to take a couple of steps first to check where his
partner is.

In this position, even at the highest level, there is often a
surprising lack of technique which needs to be rectified, and a
coach should insist that the scrum-half adopts correct foot and
body movements as he passes from the base of the scrum. The
feet need to be well apart, the body bent with the head leaning
forward over the ball to follow its flight. A twist of the hips and
flick of the wrists will then send the ball at a comfortable height to
the stand-off. Speed of service should be the priority.

Any scrum-half should be able to run through a repertoire of
moves with his loose-forward and stand-off from a scrummage or
a play-the-ball (see also pages 69 and 73), but a team must first
decide how it will best use its scrum-half's skills.

The rough and tumble type of scrum-half who might just be
lacking in that vital yard of sheer pace is often the ideal player to
act as the pivot from a play-the-ball, at, say, first or second pass
from the acting half-back. From this position he can weave,
dodge, dummy and slip passes to bigger and faster colleagues on
the break, or simply set a back division going. A quicker scrum-
half with a flair for spotting a gap and the ability to dart through it
can be deployed further along the line to feed off short passes
from a ball-playing forward, or simply to follow a tall, long-
striding second-row when close to the line. The incisive
individual break from the base of the scrum is too rarely seen.

The scrum-half can be used in the first line of defence where his
terrier-like qualities often disrupt a side and his speed off the
mark can pick up a sloppy pass. There is now, however, a tendency to play him as a 'sweeper', about ten metres behind the play
and in front of the full-back, where his job is to head off any
midfield break. Though this technique would seem to help create
overlaps for the opposition—there is one less player in the front
line—there is much to be said for the practice since a scrum-half
in this role can often use his speed and quick thinking to tackle an
attacker from the side immediately a break has been made.

Stand-off

A stand-off should be an instinctive footballer possessing sound hands allied to a sharp, tactical, footballing brain—he is the pivot who launches the free running of the threequarters. He must have a perfect understanding with his scrum-half because he has to be able to time his run on to the ball from either a short or long pass. The depth and alignment of his run are all-important, particularly if he is attempting to beat his opposite number by a sidestep or swerve, or going for the gap outside the stand-off in an effort to draw the inside centre. His skill at taking and giving a pass in one movement while running at the defenders as he straightens the line is a vital factor in creating space for the wing.

As with the scrum-half, a stand-off can adopt one of two roles, dependent upon his physique and skills. He can be the ball

20. The stand-off is one of the key players in any side and should be able to dictate the tactics of his team. The Warrington and Great Britain stand-off, Ken Kelly, likes to distribute the ball quickly to his team-mates.

distributor and general motivator in open play for the rest of the team, or he can be a finisher of movements using his pace to outstrip the opposition. Few stand-offs seem to combine both roles.

Many stand-offs, because of their physique or mental attitude, often feel disinclined to tackle, but a coach must instil into his player that he is the first point of defence from a scrummage and as such he must move up on his opposite number to tackle him or at least force him back inside into the hands of the loose-forward or breaking scrum-half. A stand-off of great pace can shadow his opposite number and run him into a colleague, or make sure he crowds out the opposite centre. When the attacking stand-off has passed the ball, the defending stand-off should continue along the line behind his centres to cover a break from a full-back or a grubber kick through the line. When the line movement is complete he can drift back into the line of defence.

THE FORWARDS

A forward must be primarily an athlete with as many individual skills as his illustrious colleagues in the backs. The Australians and New Zealanders have demonstrated in recent seasons that there can be no place in a pack for the seventeen-stone forward whose stomach overhangs his shorts and who has the licence merely to plod from scrum to scrum on the assumption that, say, at open-side prop, he wins the ball. Now there are on average only sixteen to seventeen scrums per game, he needs to do much more in loose play, though his role as a scrummager is still important. His less demanding tackling role must be complemented by greater mobility round the field.

If a team has a sixteen-stone forward who can run like a gazelle, then he must be played, because his stature is obviously ideal. But the tendency now is to include faster men of lesser bulk than forwards once were. The balance between size and speed is a delicate one and coaches should not be too dogmatic about which way the scales tip. Nevertheless they should still aim to cultivate 'the fast big 'un' as opposed to the 'fast little 'un'.

Traditional English forward play has been built up to suit the unlimited-tackle law of previous generations, whereby the six forward players had to fill set requirements: a scrummaging open-side prop of vast bulk; a ball-winning hooker who was

21. Forwards can no longer be simply the 'grafters' in a side; they must be involved in all aspects of play. A fast, heavy forward can cause havoc in defence, as Eric Chisnall (Leigh and Great Britain), here playing for St Helens, proves as his speed takes Salford by surprise.

skilful round the play-the-ball; a crafty and skilful ball-distributing prop who could despatch players upfield by spraying all manner of delicate passes; a tackling second-row and a running second-row; and a shrewd footballer at loose-forward. Such a blend was perfect for the League game then, and one invariably aimed for by many generations of coaches.

One forward tends to be the 'setter up' of all movements. With an unlimited number of tackles it was difficult to stop a well balanced combination from steamrollering on. Now with only six tackles before a possible loss of possession, there is a greater need for everyone to be able to distribute the ball, to tackle and to run.

The Australians have all their big forwards running off anyone with the ball and do not depend on one skilful ball-handler. They are all fit athletes; they all tackle and run straight at their opponents before turning and slipping the ball to an accompanying player who is supporting at speed. Consequently, there is no central point from which all attacks stem, and because of this greater variety no one player can be blotted out. So what should be demanded of our forwards in loose play and what positions should they take up on the pitch? (For other forward skills see page 62 onwards.)

In Attack

The Props and Hooker normally occupy the centre of the field during attacking loose play so they can support a threequarter move coming in from the left or right and finish it off with a try close to the posts. Sometimes, though, the front three will have to operate in the narrow area by the touchline and it is essential then that they remain close to the ball. A close-passing movement of the biggest and strongest players can batter its way through the staunchest of defences even in a confined space. But the players should not monopolize the ball and it should be passed down the line when needed.

It is a good idea to have one of the second-rows supporting the props in the event of a break, because the ball has to be moved much faster when it comes into the open. However, having said this, there is the important surprise element of a large prop taking a short pass on the burst from an outside centre which can be devastating, and one prop should be encouraged to 'float out' along the line occasionally to pick up such a pass.

The Second-Row is usually faster than the front-three and should position himself as fourth man along from the play-the-ball. Apart from making the odd straight dash down the middle, he usually runs from depth behind or accompanied by a half-back. So he must anticipate a short pass and burst on to the ball down the outside of the field, having the speed to draw an opponent and create a gap, or the strength to brush past a weak-tackling defender. He must have the instinct to know where to enter the line and not get in the way of his back line. Half-backs and second-rows should hunt together and prey off each other, and each should be at the other's shoulder when a gap has been created.

If a team is in possession of the ball in its own 22-metre area, it is often best for second-rows to take the first one or two passes at play-the-balls on a diagonal run from the midfield towards the touchlines, the play therefore being pushed to the blind-side. After this the next couple of passes can be taken more directly forward by the props. This combination will allow the kicker on the sixth tackle to have more scope for finding touch and it also takes play away from the danger area beneath the goalposts, where penalties and drop-goals can be kicked more easily.

The Loose-Forward, by nature a creative footballer who is possibly a shade too slow to play in the backs, must be allowed to rove in attack. He should be sufficiently skilled and fast enough to adopt any role, whether in close-quarter work at the scrummage or at a play-the-ball in setting up a move with his half-backs and forwards. He must be able to keep his head and assess what is going on round him so he can then make the right incursion into the line. At times this might even mean running right out to the flanks in conjunction with the centre and wing. He has much to do in varying the movements and switching play to either side of the pitch as well as helping his side to switch to a different style of play should conditions or the opposition warrant it. A thinker is needed and young players will only develop this ability over a period of time.

In Defence

All forwards must be able and eager to tackle and stand their ground in a defensive line, and drive back their opposition. In loose-play their role is to help plug any defensive gap in the line, while from a play-the-ball they should use pincer positioning to put a clamp on the opposition. Though a difficult defensive manoeuvre for schools, it is well worth trying at all levels.

As in diagram 7, the two strongest tacklers in the pack should take up a position either side of the play-the-ball and move diagonally inwards to contain the area of movement of the intended first receiver of the ball. The hooker and the man marking the play-the-ball should veer outwards in opposite directions to restrict movement even further. Two other forwards, usually the faster ones, should come up on the fringes in the event of the ball being passed, while the last forward, usually the loose-forward, should hover wide on the open-side where a team would normally be taking the ball, with a view to breaking up any movement to the backs. He can also cover back quickly to cut off a surprise break. All forwards must move eagerly and vigorously forward once the ball has been played by the foot at the play-the-ball and must never wait for the opposition to arrive.

Diagram 7.   Pincer Defence at Play-the-ball

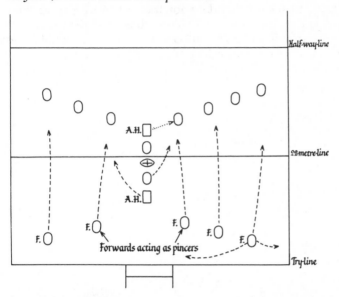

22. All forwards must be solid tacklers. Glyn Shaw (Wigan, Wales and Great Britain), here playing for Widnes, is ready to drive into his opponent, who just manages to pass the ball in time.

In any team, there needs to be a forward who thrives on tackling to set the standard for the rest to live up to. He will provide the spirit and motivation which inspires the rest when they begin to flag. And he will create the pride and stubborness in defence which often decides the result of a game.

4. Team Skills and Tactics

The unlimited-tackle law, which enabled a side to remain in possession of the ball until they committed an infringement, was changed by administrators who believed that the game had become too stereotyped. Teams were able to over-rely on one style of play in which they could use a couple of players, usually forwards, to monopolize possession. Few worried whether a move was successful as long as the team still retained possession of the ball at the end. The result was that opponents had to endure long bouts of tackling. It is no wonder that at times the play was often boring and negative with the result being more important than the means of achieving it. While not denying that the result is all-important, the style in which it is attained is important too. Under the unlimited-tackle law, attacks could be built up gradually and a team need only seriously attack in their opponents' 22-metre area. Now, with the six-tackle law, attacks can originate from anywhere on the field and there is a greater sense of urgency about the team in possession.

With only six tackles at a team's disposal, no side can afford to absorb too many tackles in negative and unproductive play. If a couple of tackles are wasted something positive must be done on the third or fourth with the emphasis on a varied approach to the play. A side now does not have the time to become too stereotyped. All its rugby must be purposeful, and behind any team's style of play there must be a design and discipline which fits in with the strengths and weaknesses of the particular team. Yet all coaches should endeavour to graft that little extra flair and skill on to the basics, especially at the play-the-ball.

It is obvious that teams will employ tactics which suit the personalities who make up the sides and that whatever skills an individual may have will have to be merged into the overall tactics of the unit whether backs or forwards. Though a style of play needs to be evolved to cover all situations in a game and to cover all the strengths and weaknesses of each player, a coach should not be content to adopt the same tactics and pattern of play on all occasions. For League to be attractive to players and spectators it must have excitement and exhibit flair from its players both individually and collectively.

Even if a coach is successful with a squad of limited talent, he must always seek to widen his team's horizons by bringing out hidden abilities in his players. He must encourage youngsters to develop their skills and to play a more open and expansive game when they are brought into the team. Though all sides must have a basic method to see them through a match, they must never be slaves to their tactics for it is flair and finesse which will raise a team to the heights and bring a crowd to fever pitch. A fine balance is required, and if a coach can introduce the unorthodox and the unexpected to methods of play in an effort to prevent monotony, so much the better.

THE SCRUM

It is one of the regrettable aspects of League that the individual and collective skills of the scrummage have declined considerably over the past few seasons. The laws relating to the scrum have

23. Poor scrummaging has marred the League game. It results particularly from the practice of the open-side prop remaining almost upright in the scrum, as demonstrated in this scrummage during the 1981 Warrington v. Widnes Challenge Cup semi-final.

24. Poor scrummaging can also result from the second-row forwards packing down incorrectly. In the Blackpool v. New Zealand match in 1980 the Blackpool second-row are seen packing down far too high and have ridden up over the backs of their front-row. This could have been avoided if they had packed down under the buttocks of the props and hooker, when pushing with a straight back would have given a more effective shove.

been far too loosely applied and referees have been over-generous with the advantage rule although they now insist on a closer adherence to the laws.

This decline in scrummaging has diverted coaches' attention from the original purpose of a scrummage, which was for both packs to push against each other to win the ball. Referees, administrators and players have been too easily influenced by the call for 'continuity of play' to such an extent that to some people scrummaging is an unnecessary interference in the flow of open play. But the scrummage is an integral part of the game and without it forwards would lose their true role and the game would suffer as a spectacle.

The methods of scrummaging advocated here keep within a strict interpretation of the laws, though sadly the techniques described will not always be the ones you will see in the professional game. However, if more attention is given to the development of correct skills at schoolboy and youth levels, and helped by the Rugby League's determination to apply the scrummaging laws strictly, then play at the scrum in the professional game should improve dramatically.

Mechanics of the Scrum

A scrum is usually made up of two packs of six forwards (see diagram 8). Each pack consists of three players in the front-row who by interlocking their arms and heads with their opponents form a clear tunnel at right angles to the touchline. The hooker, in the middle of the two props, must bind with his arms over the shoulders of those supporting him. The failure of the hooker to bind properly is the root cause of most scrum problems. Two second-row forwards will pack down, bound together by their arms entwining each other's body, in the spaces between the front-three, while the loose-forward will pack down in the space provided by the second-rows. The bodies of all the forwards should be horizontal.

Diagram 8. Set Scrummage

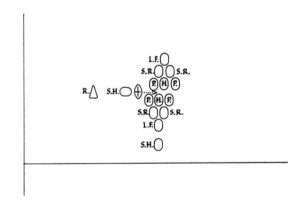

The scrum-half must feed the ball into the centre of the tunnel either by 'a downward throw from not above waist high, or by rolling it along the ground'. The ball is put into the scrum on the side of the attacking loose-head prop; and it is here where the referee will stand. The defending scrum-half has the put in, while his opposite number stays behind his own forwards.

When the scrummage has been correctly formed and the forwards have been allowed to push, the hooker will strike for the ball with either foot once it has made contact with the ground in the centre of the tunnel. A good strike from the hooker, accompanied by the necessary force in the push from the rest of the forwards, will ensure that the ball emerges correctly between and behind the inner feet of the second-row forwards.

Hooking the Ball

Far too much emphasis has been given to the art of swinging the scrum round by means of a semi-wheel in order to allow the hooker to gain a better position for a strike at the ball. With the only constraint placed upon the hooker being that his feet must be in line with his props on his side of the scrum (not even 'in a pushing position' as in Rugby Union), he often has his body bent so that he is almost facing the incoming ball. Often he attempts to corkscrew his body across the tunnel, block the opposing hooker, and then retrieve the ball with his foot or even knee. It is therefore usual for the open-side prop to pick up any deflection with his leg and steer the ball through to the second-row. This manoeuvre tends to collapse many scrums as forces are being exerted in opposite directions in the front-row. A collapsing scrum is dangerous; it is ugly to look at and rarely does the ball come back cleanly so the scrum-half can feed his backs quickly. This situation could be rectified if there is a return to solid pushing when the ball is put in. Given an effective strike by the hooker, the correct shove will see the remainder of the pack go over the ball as it exerts its force and sends the opposition pack backwards. The hooker should try to hook the ball immediately it touches the ground, or as it rises on the bounce. He needs merely to deflect the ball to the gap alongside his prop.

It is obvious then that to achieve this solid, pushing platform for the hooker, the key to cohesion and stability will lie in the grip, the bodily positioning and the foot placements of each individual in the pack working as a combined unit.

Scrummaging Positions

Front-Row   The two props and the hooker must grip each other as tightly as possible so that they form a solid front-row. At the same time as pushing at their opposite numbers, the two props should also attempt to exert inward pressure on their hooker and against the opposition hooker. This, coupled with the force of the second-rows, transmits all the push behind their own hooker at the expense of the opposing one. To achieve a solid push, the two props should have their legs well back with their feet splayed apart. Their backs should be straight and horizontal to the ground so that all the force exerted through their bodies is carried through to the opposite scrum. Their knees should be slightly bent and poised for a snap shove when the ball is put in. The common practice in professional matches of the open-side prop remaining almost upright in the scrum to give the hooker a better sight of the ball and greater manoeuvrability in twisting his body is illegal and is not to be condoned if we are ever to achieve correct scrummaging. In the upright position it is physically impossible to push to any effect. Pushing merely disrupts the scrummage.

Second-Rows As with the front-row, the second-rows should operate as a sub-unit of the pack. Before entering the scrum, they should stand a little way behind it and bind themselves tightly together by locking their arms round each other's backs. They should approach the front-row with their heads held up as this will aid the arching of the back when they insert their heads into the gaps between the hooker and props. It will also help to transmit a better shove to the props. If the head is inclined downwards in the scrummage, there is a tendency to transmit the pressure downwards to the ground, resulting in an ineffective push. It can also cause a second-row to slip down the legs of the prop in front so causing the scrum to collapse.

The second-rows should enter the scrum by aiming at the back of their props' knees with their shoulders. This will allow them to raise their shoulders snugly under the buttocks of the props. If they make impact with the buttocks there is often a tendency for them to ride over the top, so the shoulders have little to push on. When in position they should bind on to the front-row by placing their outer arms round their hips and not, as is the practice in Union, grip the front band of the shorts from beneath and between the legs. Because there are no wing-forwards, the props in League find it difficult to exert inward pressure on the hooker, a necessary factor in keeping a tight bind, so they have to be helped by the second-row binding their arms around the front-row's hips.

For an effective push both feet must be set well back and

splayed apart to obtain a good grip and a steady platform from which to launch the shove. The practice of having the outer leg back and the inner leg forward to help with the heel of the ball is not recommended for this means that strength and shove is only transmitted through one half of the body and the balance on the feet is not as sound. Nor is there any need to assist with the heel of the ball, because if the legs have been bent correctly at the knees and the snap shove timed properly then the second-rows will only have to step over the ball. With one leg forward there is often the problem of kicking the ball back through the scrum after a fast strike and deflection by the hooker and his prop.

Loose-Forward   The loose-forward should approach the scrum in exactly the same way as the second-rows. He should also have both his legs back with similar foot placings, and should bind his arms round the hips of his two colleagues in front. This binding will again help to tighten the unit and make the whole scrummage as compact as possible. He should use both legs to assist the exit of the ball from the scrum by guiding it either to the near side or far side of the scrum according to the scrum-half's wishes. Such control is vital, as is knowing when to leave the scrum when working a move with the scrum-half (see also page 69).

It is only with the aid of constant practice that a pack can operate as an effective unit and be able to time their push correctly. Therefore, coaches should give more emphasis to the art of scrummaging in their sessions, by allowing time to push against another pack or scrummage machine—revolutionary though it might be to some. The importance of scrummaging must be reaffirmed and for this to happen the attitude of coaches, players and spectators will have to be changed.

Moves from the Scrum

As the average number of scrums per match has declined in recent seasons, so has the movement of play from them. Many teams are now content to look upon scrums merely as a means of winning the ball, and too many coaches are content to see their scrum-half tackled at the base of the scrum as long as he has secured possession. Likewise, a lot of scrum-halves have forgotten the basic priority of their position—that of passing the ball to the stand-off. Consequently, coaches and players need to adopt a more positive attitude in this area and realize that the scrum is not only a means of winning the ball, but is also a base for launching attacks while all the fast-covering forwards are conveniently tucked away.

Admittedly, there are times when, say, a scrum is close to the try-line with the need for the defending scrum-half to retain the ball once it has emerged. In these circumstances, he will be content to take the tackle in order to make it safe to play the ball to his forwards after the scrum has broken up. This is an obvious way for a team to move out of the danger zone of their 22-metre area, but in most other circumstances a good clean service from the base of the scrum is what is required.

There is an unlimited number of attacking ploys to use behind a scrum, and there is no finer sight for a crowd than to see the ball being fanned along the back line at speed and out to a winger who is put clear of the cover. The game needs more of these purposeful moves but, as at the play-the-ball, the attacks must be varied and balanced—some from close in and others from wide out.

25. For any attacking move from the scrum to be successful, the scrum-half and loose-forward must know almost instinctively what the other is going to do. When scrum-half Mike Lampkowski (Wakefield Trinity) drives on the blind-side from the back of the scrum and is covered by Doug Laughton (Widnes and Great Britain), Lampkowski's loose-forward is already breaking from the scrum to lend support.

Attacking from the Scrum

Scrum-Half and Loose-Forward Combinations A close understanding between the scrum-half and loose-forward is vital to
any side. And a successful combination can create many scoring
chances from the base of the scrum using numerous ploys. The
players must practise their moves until they become instinctive
and their understanding becomes second nature. If a scrum-half
breaks from the scrum, for example, he should be able to take for
granted that his loose-forward will be on hand to take an inside
pass. Likewise the scrum-half must be alert to the loose-forward
picking the ball up as it comes back from the second-row and

26. Alternatively, a loose-forward such as Harold Pinner (St Helens and
Great Britain) will be prepared to take the ball from the scrum and break
down the blind-side before linking with the scrum-half and wing.

27. Because the forwards are occupied in a scrummage, possession from the heel enables a side to set up an attack while there is plenty of open space on the pitch. Like all good scrum-halves, Reg Bowden (Widnes and Fulham) quickly moves the ball away from the scrum to his stand-off, who is in a better position to initiate a move to exploit the gaps.

flicking him a pass as he loops round the back of the scrum. One trick which works well is when the scrum-half moves to the back of the scrum and bends as if to pick up the ball, shouting 'Mine'. As he does this he darts away towards the try-line without the ball. Instead, the loose-forward picks it up and drives for the try-line on the other side in the hope that the defending scrum-half and loose-forward will have been deceived into tackling the scrum-half as the decoy.

Two moves which can be worked near to the scrum involve additional co-ordination between the scrum-half and stand-off, and they are ideal for breaking down a tight defence.

Dummy Run   The scrum-half picks up the ball at the base of the scrum and gives a quick pass to the stand-off who has to stand closer and flatter to the scrum than usual (see diagram 9). He then follows the pass and runs round the stand-off who by now will have turned his back to the opposition to shield the ball. The stand-off now dummies to him as he races past and slips the ball

Diagram 9.   Dummy Run

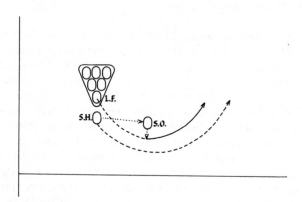

to the loose-forward who has broken from the scrum and is following the play. The loose-forward can then drive for the line knowing that he has the scrum-half scampering at his elbow should he need to beat a player with a further pass.

Winger and Full-back Break   This is a similar movement in that the scrum-half has to give a good clean service to the stand-off and then make a dummy run round him as he turns to shield the ball (see diagram 10). But instead of the loose-forward taking the ball, it is slipped to either the winger or full-back, both of whom

Diagram 10. Winger and Full-back Break

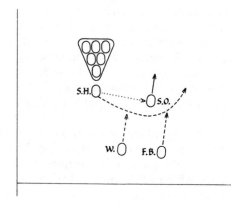

should be racing alongside him at full speed, determined to break the grip of any would-be tacklers.

There are countless moves which can be used once the ball is in the hands of the stand-off. These range from a simple 'loop move' with the stand-off passing to the inside centre and then running round to take the return pass, to a full scissors movement. Here the stand-off will run across and in front of his inside-centre, who, having stood a little deeper than usual, will run in the opposite direction and take a reverse pass from the stand-off. A dummy scissors can be most effective when the same movement occurs, but the stand-off, instead of reverse passing to the inside-centre, dummies his pass and continues to link up with the outside-centre or the full-back coming into the line. Equally, many 'miss-moves' can be tried in which one player misses out the player next to him in the line with a long pass in an attempt to put the outside player in the clear.

Defence at the Scrum

The back-three forwards play a key role in defence at the scrum, and of these the loose-forward is the most important. Because he has to work closely with his scrum-half, both on the open-side and blind-side, a good understanding between the two is vital. Since the introduction of the law that allows the loose-forward to detach himself from the scrum, I would recommend that when he is near his own try-line he stands out of the scrum and covers an attack on the opposite side of the scrum to his scrum-half. The scrum-half, being the defending player, will be putting the ball into the scrum on the loose-head and hence will cover any break close to that side of the scrum. This will help to block all eventualities, but it has the disadvantage that it leaves the scrum one player light for the push. A coach will have to weigh the pros and cons of this before deciding whether his loose-forward should pack down or not. He can leave the scrum once the ball has been heeled by the opposition, but he must get himself quickly into a defensive position.

In general play, once a blind-side break has been covered, the loose-forward must break towards the attacking threequarter-line on the open-side of the pitch to be on hand for any inside break or scissors move which will bring play back across the field. The scrum-half should be encouraged to travel in a line behind his backs to cover the outside break or grubber kick. The two second-rows are also necessary in defence. If there is no blind-side break, the blind-side player should drop back into line to await any switch of direction, while the open-side player should cover deep behind his own back division as a last-ditch defence with the full-back and any covering blind-side winger.

THE PLAY-THE-BALL

When a player has been tackled, the act of bringing the ball into play is known as a 'play-the-ball'. It is now the vital component of the League game, taking place on average every twenty seconds, so it must be performed properly if a team is to flourish. But unless there is variety and originality in the movements stemming from it, it will degenerate into a very boring and stereotyped feature of the game. Therefore, two aspects of the play-the-ball must be encouraged to excite the spectator and to offer variety to the player—*speed* and *variation of movement* from its execution.

Mechanics of the Play-the-Ball

After a player has been tackled he has to get to his feet where he was stopped, lift the ball clear of the ground, face his opponents' try-line and drop or place the ball in front of his foot. As soon as the ball touches the ground, it may be kicked or heeled in any direction by any player, but in practice, because penalties are given for premature kicking, the player marking rarely kicks the ball and leaves the tackled player free to heel the ball.

Standing directly behind the player of the ball and the marker (as in diagram 11) are two players known as the acting half-backs. The one behind the man playing the ball is the one who usually receives the heel and starts play again. The acting half-back behind the marker usually adopts a close-tackling role as explained earlier in the pincer movement (see page 58) for defence, but many defending sides dispense with him altogether. All other players on both sides must retire five metres behind their own player taking part in the play-the-ball and must not advance until the ball has been dropped to the ground.

Since the movement is a set piece where the players of both sides stop continuous play and realign themselves for defence or

Diagram 11.

attack, speed is the priority. A clean and crisp play-the-ball must be performed quickly, with the tackled player jumping to his feet and not dawdling. A series of fast play-the-balls hardly gives a defence any respite to realign itself. When players are still retiring, a gap will soon emerge. But if the movement is performed slowly, the full defence will have time to realign and cover every available gap with a tackler. In training, a coach should simulate a game and at every tackle count aloud to three, by which time the tackled player should be on his feet and releasing the ball. Note the speed at which this game will flow and look for the vast number of gaps that will occur as defenders hastily seek to get back into position.

The need for speed and variety from a play-the-ball means that a team must have a quick-thinking ball player and sound handler in the acting half-back position when in possession of the ball. Most teams prefer a hooker who is a shrewd footballer. This has the advantage that he is used to the close forward play and knows what type of pass to give in different situations, particularly when releasing the backs to take part in open-play movements. Other sides use a half-back, often a scrum-half, to gain speed of service, at the same time as having a man who is used to changing the direction of play to take advantage of defensive weaknesses. The disadvantage in using a scrum-half, however, lies in the fact that one of the best footballers on the field is usually tied up at close quarters and is not available for open running wider out towards the wings. Only a team coach can decide the player and the priorities for his own side as he determines the style of play to be adopted.

Tactics for the Play-the-Ball

Before planning any tactics at the play-the-ball, a coach must first look at the four basic requirements for positive play:

1 The play-the-ball must be performed as fast as possible. The player of the ball must break free from the tackle and be on his feet to play the ball within seconds of being grounded or the referee calling 'Held'. The Australians are masters at not wasting time in continuing play and frequently catch opponents out of position. Coaches should concentrate on the speed of the play-the-ball in their practices of unopposed rugby and anyone dragging his feet should be despatched to the side to run a lap of the field as a penalty.

2 It must be clear who the acting half-back is to be. As mentioned, it can be the hooker or the scrum-half, but maximum advantage can be gained from having the hooker take the job in the opponents' half of the field in order to release the scrum-half for open running, while the scrum-half could take over in his own half to release the stronger and heavier hooker for clearing the try-line. Using two different players adds to the variety of the team, but there should never be any waiting for the usual acting half-back to appear, and sometimes when a long-range break has taken play to within a few metres of the opponents' try-line, any player on the spot should perform the role.

3 All players, especially the first receiver of the ball from the acting half-back, must run on to the ball from a deep position and not catch it when stationary. A player standing still has few options open to him. He will find it difficult to dummy or change direction and so will rarely be able to create a gap in a defence. Above all he slows down the movement of the team.

4 All players must be taught the virtues of backing up the player with the ball. No team can be successful unless the ball-carrier can slip a pass to a supporting team-mate at the moment he is tackled. Movements should never die through lack of support and the coach must insist on getting his players to back up a player who makes a break. Any fit side should be eager to support. Players should also get into position quickly after breaking a tackle, because there is nothing worse than to see a move flounder because a player is not where he should be.

In Possession in Defence   A team's playing tactics will obviously be suited to their position on the pitch. And though it might sound heresy to suggest that a side in possession of the ball can be in defence, a League team will try to work their way out of their 22-metre area using a series of play-the-balls just as a Union team might work their way out by using a kick to touch on the full. Both will be seeking a better position from which to attack.

Obviously when a team is on its own line there is a need for steadiness and for two or three forwards to attempt to clear the line by taking the first pass from the acting half-back and driving forward. Taking the ball to the blind-side will clear the open-side for a more fluent attack later, and in the event of an infringement any kick at goal will be well away from the posts. If the open-side of the pitch has been opened up, a good ploy is to play the two half-backs at acting half-back and first receiver to move the ball quickly to a strong-running second-row forward who can drive through on the burst. This is not an area for frills in the play, though very often as tacklers tend to crowd round the play-the-ball in an attempt to stifle play, if the defenders run on to the ball from depth and pass at speed an attack can soon develop in the centre. Very often a scrum-half, when at acting half-back, can spot a gap when the tacklers advance and can take advantage of a slack marker at the play-the-ball. Many valuable metres can be gained by a player keeping the ball to himself and darting through his opponents' line, often giving a respite to his forwards who might need a breather.

In Possession in Attack   One of the virtues of being able to retain possession in the tackle in League is that it can allow a side to attack from anywhere on the field. The non-retention of the ball in the tackle in Union can bring about a safety-first policy, so that many players kick for position rather than risk a tackle in their own half. No situation like this can occur in League. Though one of the most welcome sights in recent seasons has been the increasing use of the shrewd kick (grubber or touch-finding) to break down a tight defence, or the high kick to put pressure on an opposing team, there can be no excuse for a League team not looking for an opening anywhere outside their 22-metre area. Indeed it is worth looking for breaks inside it, because some of the finest match-winning tries are scored from this area.

At 'first receiver' from a play-the-ball, it is necessary for a team

28. Variety at the play-the-ball is vital if a team is to keep the opposition guessing what it is going to do next. Here the Salford hooker Ellis Devlin passes the ball to his scrum-half, Ken Gill, in an attempt to open play out towards the flanks.

29. Alternatively, as David Ward (Leeds and Great Britain) shows here, the acting half-back can draw in the defence round a play-the-ball before attempting to switch the direction of play.

to have a good ball distributor who can direct and switch play as the situation demands. The sooner a team escapes from an over-reliance on one ball distributor the better they will be. Just as speed at the play-the-ball movement is vital, so is the movement of the ball from the first receiver, especially if the ball is to travel along the threequarter line. This passing must complement good running on to the ball from deep positions, and this will be aided if the line is not cluttered up with too many forwards. As a general rule, the ball should never pass through more than two pairs of forwards' hands on the way to the wings. Where forwards are important is when a strong-running second-row takes a pass from a deep-lying position off a centre or a half-back as wide out as possible (see diagram 12). A strong burst in this area from such a player can lead to a devastating break. Few centres or wingers relish tackling fifteen stones on the move!

Diagram 12.

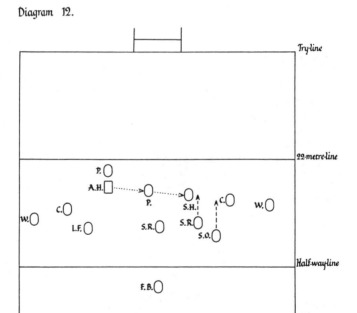

Variety is the keynote to success. If a team continually passes the ball along the line for the whole of a match, then opponents will soon find ways of counteracting their play. It is far more difficult to anticipate what is going to happen if sometimes the ball is sent out to stretch a defence, while at other times attacks are set up from close to a play-the-ball. Alternatively, a team can draw a defence into the play-the-ball by a series of close forward movements and then stretch it by quickly fanning the ball out wide. A team must always keep the defence guessing and not allow a side to anticipate where the next attack is to come from. All teams must develop moves round the play-the-ball, whether for close attacking positions near the try-line, for use in making midfield breaks, or simply for the purpose of drawing in defenders to the midfield before giving the ball to the winger to show his talents. Coaches will have to create moves to suit the players in their teams. The following three suggestions are ones which a coach might like to get straight first.

Run Around This move (see diagram 13) involves the same principles as the penalty-kick move (see page 87). The acting half-back passes the ball to the first receiver (1) and continues running round him. The receiver can then pass the ball to either of the two deep-lying forwards (2 or 3), who should drive hard on diagonal paths from behind. On his loop round he can, if he wishes, return the ball to the acting half-back, who in turn can open play out wider with a long pass to midfield or have a forward, preferably a fast moving second-row, take a short pass on the burst into a convenient gap. The receiver can dummy to all the runners and seek a gap in the defence himself.

Diagram 13. Run Around

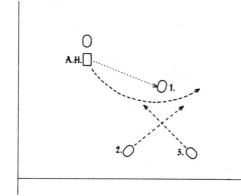

30. The run-around movement is an effective way of making an extra man in the line and thus the possibility of an overlap. Even as David Topliss (Hull and Great Britain), here playing for Wakefield Trinity, is passing the ball, he is preparing to loop around his partner to take a return pass. Alternatively, his partner can dummy to him and pass to another supporting player.

Switch of Direction Following the pass from the acting half-back to the receiver (1), the same run-around movement is performed, but the receiver passes the ball to a half-back (2) who will race across the back and over to the opposite side (see diagram

Diagram 14. Switch of Direction

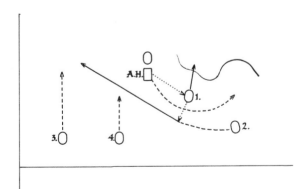

14). As he races flat, across and in front of the opponents' line, he merely has to turn so that one of the forwards (3 or 4), racing from depth, can take the ball off him. Such a move, even if unsuccessful, will draw the covering tacklers over to the blind-side and, in the event of a speedy play-the-ball, can provide opportunities for the backs on the open-side of the field.

Dummy Switch   This move is often performed near the opposition try-line and especially when the defenders are rushing up fast to stop the ball being passed along the line. On receiving the ball, the acting half-back must flick it upwards, directly through his legs, to enable the forward, positioned at (1), to take it as he moves across and behind him (see diagram 15). As the forward plunges for the try-line, the acting half-back drives for the line on the open-side without the ball in an attempt to draw the tacklers and leave the try-line exposed.

Diagram 15. Dummy Switch

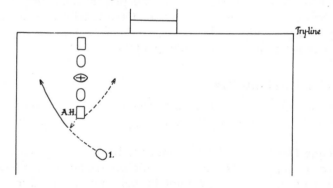

Without Possession in Defence   Having already considered the need for a pincer defence and noted the advantages of a sweeper, a coach must insist that immediately the ball touches the ground at a play-the-ball everyone eagerly moves forward to tackle. This will limit the time and space available to a player on the attack. Defenders must never stand flat-footed and wait for the runner with the ball. They should be alert, on their toes and hungry to 'take out' the attacker with the ball.

KICKING

Although League is essentially a ball-handling game, kicking is still an important element which if used effectively can bring a new dimension to a team's play. Yet it is becoming a neglected art particularly at the start of a game or the restart of play after a stoppage, in other words from 'dead ball' situations. On these occasions, the team with the ball have a tremendous advantage in that they can organize themselves and dictate where the ball goes without pressure from the opposition. So these opportunities should not be wasted. For example, one of the least constructive features of the game is the number of kick-offs and drop-outs that are aimlessly kicked upfield. There seems to be little co-ordination between the kicker and his support players, who hardly make any attempt to retrieve the ball or put pressure on the opposition. This is something to which a coach should pay more attention. He should insist that the kicker puts the opposition under pressure even though they gain possession of the ball, or that he directs his kick to give the players following up a half-chance of regaining possession. Occasionally it is worth trying a surprise move which, say, after a short kick allows the ball to be swept up and a handling attack started.

Kicks from the Half-Way-Line

Kicks from the half-way-line are made to start each half of the game and to restart play after a score.

The Long Deep Kick   There is much to be said for such a kick towards the opponents' corner flag and in-goal area as it allows the kicker's side to start the game in their opponents' 22-metre area—especially if the support players rush into the tackle quickly enough. The ball should be kicked with considerable force, possibly from an unorthodox placing, and not too high, so that any player fielding it might be forced to deal with an awkward bounce at the same time as receiving the oncoming tacklers who will also be trying to cut down his area of movement. If the following five tackles are made correctly there will be a scrum and, with the loose-head of the scrum going to the attacking side, the team who kicked-off should be able to establish a quick territorial advantage.

To counteract such a tactic, the receiving side can swing the ball away from the touchline and the oncoming forwards to the mid-field by means of quick interpassing and sure handling. An attack can therefore be launched immediately towards the other flank where a half-back or winger might be able to prise an opening. A sensible attacking side, however, will position three forwards on either side of the kicker, five metres behind the half-way-line (see diagram 16). They will start to run as soon as the kicker moves to kick the ball, and will be in full flight when he makes contact so they can quickly put pressure on the opposition. Such a line up does not give the defending side any indication as to where the ball is to be kicked and it enables the kicking side to have suffi-cient tackling cover if their opponents switch the ball to midfield.

Diagram 16.

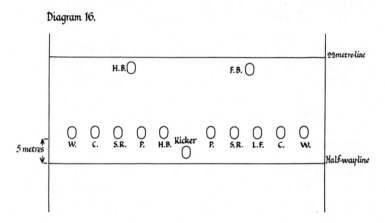

In Australian Rugby League a current tactic being used against a deep kick which pins a team almost on its own line is for the full-back to make a high and deep return kick behind the oncom-ing tacklers. Although this loses possession, it isolates the oppo-sition full-back and places him under pressure as would-be tack-lers break out from their defensive positions, taking care not to infringe the offside law. This tactic is in favour with Australian teams because their tackling is often so tight and dependable that they prefer to give the ball away to contain the opposition in their own half.

Kicking for the 10-Metre-Line   There is nothing so infuriating as seeing a kicker delicately lift a ball to drop on the 10-metre-line only for his team to follow up at half-pace, giving their opponents the time and space to collect and move the ball away from trouble. The aim of such a kick is to try to regain possession so ball and forwards should arrive on the 10-metre-line together. This takes practice to perfect and players should not forget that they are working for each other. The kicker must try to get the ball to 'hang' in the air to give his forwards time to get up on it. And likewise they should follow up at speed eager to get their hands on the ball.

A good way of regaining possession is to group the forwards in a two and four formation on one side of the centre-line. The two tallest forwards should be about five metres behind the line and the other four about ten metres behind. At the kick all six will be moving towards the receivers in the hope that the two tallest forwards can leap to catch the ball or tap it back into the hands of one of the four forwards following up. Remember that the receivers are endeavouring to make a good catch—all the pressure is on them. The 'tappers' have little to worry about save leaping high at the ball as it drops. This can be a most successful ploy for retrieving possession and at the least it can harass a waiting defender into knocking-on. But whichever side accidently knocks on, it is to the benefit of the kicking side, which gets the loose-head at the resulting scrum.

Variations from the Kick-Off   The willingness and confidence to try unorthodox moves marks players and teams of the highest class; and nowhere is there a better chance for keeping a receiving side on its toes than by quick thinking at the kick-off. A change of direction late in the kicker's run up can send a high ball in the opposite direction over to the unmarked winger on the other side of the field. And a short kick deliberately made to bounce along the ground for the kicker to field can often take a team by surprise or again cause a slow-thinking forward to knock-on or lose the ball in panic. Variations, however, are only surprises when tried once or at the most twice in a match and should be reserved for special occasions. Remember also never to kick towards a renowned danger man!

The defending team should of course be well spaced to cover as much of the field as possible. The actual receiver of the ball must shout 'Mine' as the ball approaches in order to avoid confusion or even collision with a colleague. The line-up has been fairly standard over the years (see diagram 17), with the forwards taking the

Diagram 17.

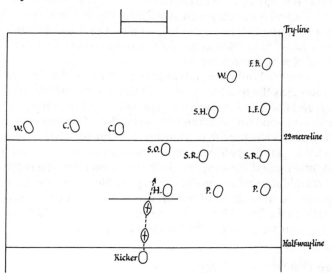

side of the field where the ball is expected to be kicked and the backs covering the other half, ever alert for the beginning of a quick attacking movement. It is worthwhile retaining this formation though I would change the customary positions of the wing and full-back. The full-back is the better catcher and fielder of the ball under pressure and hence should be nearer the touchline, while the quicker man, the wing, if he takes the ball in midfield can round an opponent the more easily and perhaps help to start an attacking movement. One of the two half-backs should be positioned near the forwards on the chance of receiving a quick pass and thereby being able to start a passing movement. It also puts him in a good position to act quickly at a play-the-ball if a forward is tackled.

Drop-Out from the Try-Line

When a defending player has to restart the game with a drop-out from the centre of his own try-line, he must be extremely careful where he puts the kick, even though the options available are very limited. The long kick, booted upfield with great force, but with little thought, can often result in the defending side being placed under greater pressure than before the drop-out. It is obvious though that the kicker must put the ball as far upfield as possible to take the play well away from the try-line. He should also give some height to the ball to give the defenders time to move upfield as quickly as possible to put pressure on the catcher and cut down his movements.

The kicker should aim towards the centre of the field rather than towards the touchlines to avoid kicking the ball directly into touch and therefore giving away a penalty in front of the posts. A ball kicked wide towards the wings could be dangerous as there are fewer tacklers here than there are in midfield. The kicker must also try to put the ball in a space where a player can be isolated with little immediate support. So to counteract this, the receiving side should spread out as deeply as possible to face the kick and be prepared to switch and run off the catcher at speed as soon as he gathers the ball. Many a try can be scored by a sudden switch of direction which takes the tacklers by surprise.

Drop-Out from the 22-Metre-Line

When the ball is kicked out of play over the dead-ball-line or the touch-in-goal-line from a penalty kick and is not touched by any player other than the kicker, a drop-out will be given from the 22-metre-line. From here a similar kick to that described above can be used, but teams should also look to work the blind-side to add some variation to their play. Very often a change of direction can find a gap on the opposite side of the field through which the ball can roll into touch, or, if the tacklers are not marked properly, a neatly lobbed kick into the arms of the winger following up the kick can be most effective. And a kick taken quickly can often gain many metres while the opposition are still regrouping.

A Place Kick on the 22-Metre-Line

When restarting play at the 22-metre-line, it is customary for the kicker merely to tap the ball to himself and thereby retain possession for his team. However, a team should not forget that occasionally, perhaps in the dying seconds of a match played in bad weather, it might be better to kick the ball far upfield and play in their opponents' half despite the lack of possession. But with the opposition forced to retire ten metres from the ball most teams will try to clear their 22-metre-area with two or three direct probes from large forwards. Such forwards hope to gain five or ten metres at every dash and once they have moved from the danger zone, the backs are then brought into play on the final two tackles. Simple, direct driving by the forwards can be useful if a team has been under intense pressure, because it will allow a side to compose itself and gain breathing space. The use of six tackles by a team in such a situation can take the edge off any previous intensive attacking pressure. The kicker of the ball, on playing it to himself, can very often gain many metres without passing it to a colleague if he darts away quickly.

A more adventurous side, however, would be recommended to use a hooker to tap the ball through the centre of the 22-metre-line, and then pass it to the two half-backs (see diagram 18). Ultimately, a strong-running forward coming through on the burst should take the ball about thirty metres from the original kick where there is usually the greatest concentration of tacklers. Such quick handling, allowing for the necessary ten-metre gap between tacklers and runners, can often achieve a break further out in the centre positions.

Diagram 18.

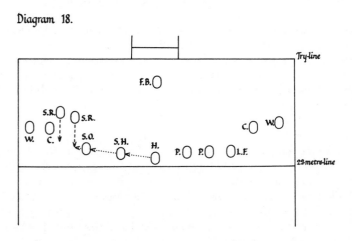

Penalty Kick

Whenever a penalty kick has been awarded, the non-offending side may take the kick by punting, drop-kicking or place-kicking the ball from any point on or behind the mark and parallel to the touchline. If a kick at goal is not to be taken, a player can gain a quick advantage for his team by tapping the ball forward through the mark and playing it to himself while the opponents are still retreating and regrouping their defences. Such quick thinking by a player can create a gap close to the try-line which may lead to a score. Alternatively, the ball can be tapped quickly and passed through three or four pairs of hands to set up an attack on the flanks before the offending side have recovered. Therefore, a clever, nippy, half-back should never waste a second when the whistle has gone.

If a team prefer to gain ground and secure territorial advantage by kicking to touch this will result in the kicking side restarting play with a free kick. Usually the kicker will tap the ball forward and retrieve it himself, but teams should try to add variety to their play by devising moves to outwit the opposition. For example, a team can sometimes draw in the opposition by using three forwards in turn to drive at the defence. This is followed by a fast play-the-ball and quick passing of the ball across the line to open space, hopefully now lacking in covering forwards. Unfortunately, too many teams waste tackles in this area of play but this should not prevent them from trying to be more adventurous in using pre-planned moves. There are many moves a coach can use. Those described below will cause any would-be tacklers to think and, if worked successfully, can provide the required breakthrough in a tight defence. Yet schoolmasters should never feel that such moves are too difficult for their boys and they should use them to push a young player to the limits of his skill and thinking.

Run Around   This move can provide at least three options for attack (see diagram 19). The scrum-half, normally a quick runner and sure handler, should tap the ball forward, retrieve it and pass to his colleague (1) standing about five metres away, who then shields the ball by turning his back to the opposition. The receiver is now in a position to dictate the play. He can dummy to the scrum-half as he follows his pass round and then flick the ball to the forward (3) bursting through on his outside. Alternatively, he can pass the ball to player 2, while the scrum-half runs round both men, and player 2 can then set the ball up for player 4 dashing through at speed. A third option is for player 2 to return the ball to the scrum-half as he runs past and he will then open out play to another player coming on the burst. He can even initiate a passing movement across field away from the concen-

Diagram 19. Run Around

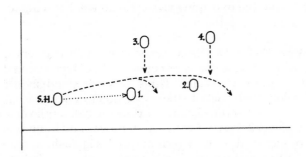

tration of tacklers. For these moves to be successful, it is essential that each player times his run accurately. The scrum-half should pass the pivot (1 or 2) just before the support forward arrives so that it makes it difficult for the opposition to know who is going to take the ball.

The Switch Play can be cleverly transferred from the open-side to the blind-side, where an attack can be launched down the touchline, using a switch move (see diagram 20). The line-up is basically the same as for 'Run Around' with the addition of two players on the blind-side. When player 1 receives the ball, he waits for the scrum-half to go past as a decoy and then throws a pass in the opposite direction to player 5. He immediately slips it

Diagram 20. Switch

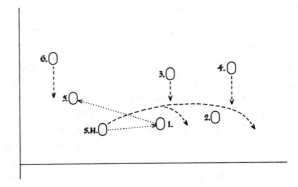

to player 6 who could possibly be a strong winger in full flight. Again, for this move to be successful the ball must be passed at speed to avoid the oncoming tacklers who will be trying to close down the man with the ball.

Three-Man Wall This is a clever move which offers a few options when close to the opponents' try-line. I have seen it well worked by Australian teams. Three forwards stand shoulder to shoulder with their backs to the opposition to shield the ball (see diagram 21). The scrum-half must pass the ball to player 1 who slips it to player 2. Player 3 will then step away and leave a gap of a couple of metres through which player 4 will dash, at the same time receiving a short pass, and then plunge for the try-line.

Diagram 21. Three-man Wall

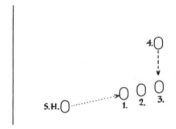

Alternatively, the ball can be transferred to player 3 and then passed back to the scrum-half if he follows round his original pass. The scrum-half can then give the ball to player 4 running either inside or outside him. A third option is for player 3 to dummy a pass to player 4 as he runs through the inside gap and then peel off himself towards the try-line.

Differential Penalty

The differential penalty operates for technical offences at the scrum, and a team can elect to kick and use one of the above ploys. But the scrum-half or loose-forward must always have his wits about him to see whether a quick tap of the ball through the mark will be effective. While the offending team are disorganized, he might give his side a great advantage by bringing the ball into play again before the opposition expect it. Never forget that a planned move can still be carried out among the backs with the advantage that the opposition are retreating and the scrum-half is often unhindered by his opponent.

Tactical Kicking in Open Play

As I indicated earlier, tactical kicking now plays a greater part in League, although it is not used to the extent it is in Union. It can be used most effectively as a variation from the usual forms of attack and defence. If a team has the wind at their backs, they are going to benefit territorially from some well directed kicks. Likewise, if playing down a slope, a good kick can force the opposition back to their line where they will have to work hard to break out up the slope. A team with fast wingers can also benefit from kicking deep to the flanks where the wingers can follow up at speed to pressurize their opposite numbers. And if the hooker is winning a majority of scrums then a team can kick deep into the opposition half, say, on the second or third play-the-ball, make the six tackles and be fairly confident of winning the ball back at the ensuing scrum.

There is no disgrace in kicking the ball as deep as possible if your team has a weak defence and there are doubts about their ability to make six tackles near their own line. It is better to clear your opponents to the half-way-line and hope to absorb the tackles in a less dangerous area.

Unlike Union, tactical kicking is not usually the preserve of one or two players; the coach must ensure that all thirteen men are proficient in this aspect of play.

5. Off the Field – the Correct Approach

Virtually every League player who takes the field, professional as well as amateur, does so because he enjoys playing the game. Despite the fatigue, pain and disappointment, week in, week out, hundreds of teams compete against each other at all levels, everyone striving to win a league or a cup. And for a small club taking a trophy, success can be as satisfying as for a professional club winning the Challenge Cup at Wembley.

To get the most out of the game, it must be approached in the right spirit. Enjoyment is lessened if coaches and players adopt a casual or slipshod manner. Few people, particularly youngsters, enjoy being continually defeated and players will soon lose interest and give up playing unless they can see some improvement in their own play and that of their team. But success does not come easily and has to be worked for, and it will be founded on a determination to win, a desire to learn, and the character to persevere when all is not going well.

A coach has a vital role to play in creating in a team or club an atmosphere which players will respond to. He must be a good tactician able to adapt the style of play to suit the abilities and ages of his players. If he has a good strong pack, for example, he must play to it. Clever, tricky backs he should use wisely, and if he has a sound kicker he should be given full advantage of any wind or slope, and used to aid a weak defence with relieving kicks. The coach must lead by example and be able to convey his enthusiasm for the game.

Training sessions should be organized and properly structured in order to reflect the needs of the team and individuals, not just for one training night, but for the season as a whole. Yet a coach must be prepared to adapt and change as circumstances alter. A typical session will vary enormously according to the ages, abilities and attitudes of the players. Training sessions that are dull and monotonous will fail to encourage flair and skill as players become bored with uninteresting routines. In contrast, properly constructed sessions will bring out the best in talented players and possibly enable a team's tactics to be built round them. Unless a player is stretched physically and mentally in training, he will not be able to respond to the challenges that arise in a match.

Rugby is a running game, hence any improvement in a player's basic speed is essential. Training, therefore, must include running, but it is important to remember that many exercises, those described in the preceding chapters, for example, involve ball handling as well, so it is possible to bring a satisfying mixture of activities to a training session.

Developing fitness is an essential ingredient of training sessions, particularly in the run-up to the start of a new season and for the first few games. Unless a player is fit, he cannot fully participate in a game. If a player is gasping for breath before half-time, he is of little use to his side and is unlikely to be enjoying the game. Many players shy away from the 'torture' of fitness work, so a coach must make these sessions interesting.

Apart from being fit, a player must also be in the right frame of mind when he plays in a match. A coach therefore has to help his side prepare mentally as well as physically. He has to boost their confidence and persuade them to believe in their ability so he can bring them to a peak for the crucial games in a season. To do this a coach must know his side well. He must be able to judge when he needs to put the pressure on in training and when to relax if he feels the players are becoming stale and overtrained. With some players at times he needs to be sparing while with others he has to be more demanding.

There are many different types of coach; some are quiet and softly spoken, while others are more extrovert and bellow their commands across the pitch. If he is respected for his ability then he will get the most from his players. But he must not be afraid to call in assistance to get across particular points to his team. In this the help of a well-known player invited along to a training session can be invaluable. Not only will players be able to see at first hand how techniques and skills are put into practice, but the effect of working alongside a top player can be a tremendous fillip to their confidence and enthusiasm.

As the season develops, it is a good idea for a coach and perhaps some of his players to look at other teams to assess their strengths and weaknesses prior to playing them. All teams develop a style of play which frequently revolves round certain key players and a coach should make his team aware of this and any particular moves that might be worked in certain areas of the pitch. He should then suggest ways of dealing with these situations and perhaps the eccentricities of some of the opposition players. It may mean detailing one or two of his players to do certain jobs.

I do not believe in building up a huge dossier on the opposing team and its players. It can often be counter-productive, involving coach and players spending too much time looking at the opposition and not paying enough attention to their own preparation. Too much information can inhibit a team's own style of play as they worry too much about what the opposition are likely to do. A team should have the confidence in their own ability to feel that the opposition should be afraid of them.

A worthwhile exercise when preparing for games is for a team to assess its performance in previous matches. Here a coach should point out where moves broke down and why, and he should discuss with individual players the reasons for a defensive lapse or the failure to finish an attack. Mistakes can be simulated in training so a player can see exactly where he is going wrong and he can then work on his faults and weaknesses. And a blackboard session can provide a calmer atmosphere in which players can analyse tactics and raise points about how the team is playing. These sessions could be supplemented with a film of a match or a coaching film hired from the Rugby League. These are especially useful for younger players, as a film can be stopped to highlight particular points which a coach can then explain.

Many professional and some amateur clubs use video equipment to record each game so they can analyse their play in training. Most players like to see themselves on film, but hate to see themselves make a mistake which can be highlighted in front of their team-mates in slow motion. Many schools now have video equipment, too, and as the cost of a camera can easily be raised in one good fund-raising effort, so they can also have the benefits this brings. Alternatively, a cheaper method is for a coach to use a pocket cassette to record his thoughts as a game is in progress, so he can refresh his memory when he discusses the match with his players afterwards.

There are two pieces of equipment which all teams should think seriously about obtaining—a weight-training machine and a scrummage machine. Strength is one of the key factors in League and it can be developed in regular short sessions at the end of a training session or on separate nights by using a weight-training machine. At least twelve players can work on the equipment at the same time, so it is a tremendous asset to any club or school for a relatively small outlay. It usually takes about half an hour for a player to complete his personal training schedule. He can also work on particular parts of his body to give him the extra strength he might need for his playing position.

The second piece of equipment is a scrummage machine, which is used by virtually all Union clubs. I find it incomprehensible that although the scrummage is one of the few unit techniques in the League game, it is practised very little. I do not know of any professional club which has a scrummage machine or that practises unit skills around the scrum. I am sure that if these aspects of the game were practised under the laws of League the scrum would be restored to its rightful prominence.